LUCY DANIELS

Lamb
in the
Laundry

Hodder
Children's
Books

A division of Hachette Children's Books

Special thanks to Helen Magee
Thanks also to C. J. Hall, B. Vet. Med., M.R.C.V.S. for reviewing
the veterinary information contained in this book

Animal Ark is a trademark of Working Partners Limited
Text copyright © by Ben M. Baglio 1995
Created by Ben M. Baglio, London W6 0HF
Illustrations copyright © by Shelagh McNicholas 1995

First published in Great Britain in 1995
by Hodder Children's Books
This edition published in 2007

The right of Lucy Daniels to be identified as the Author of
the Work has been asserted by her in accordance with the
Copyright, Designs and Patents Act 1988.

For more information about Animal Ark, please contact
www.animalark.co.uk

1

A Catalogue record for this book is available from the British Library

ISBN-13: 978 0 340 94444 8

Typeset in Baskerville by Avon DataSet Ltd,
Bidford-on-Avon, Warwickshire

Printed and bound in Great Britain by
Clays Ltd, St Ives plc

The paper and board used in this paperback by Hodder Children's
Books are natural recyclable products made from wood grown in
sustainable forests. The manufacturing processes conform to the
environmental regulations of the country of origin.

Hodder Children's Books
a division of Hachette Children's Books
338 Euston Road, London NW1 3BH
An Hachette Livre UK company

One

'Ready?' said Mr Hope.

'Just coming,' Mandy replied, smiling at her dad. 'Blackie wants to carry the picnic basket.'

Mr Hope grinned. 'So long as he doesn't eat all the food,' he said.

'Even Blackie couldn't manage all that,' said James. He pushed his glasses up his nose and bent down to Blackie. Blackie was James's Labrador. 'Put it down, Blackie,' he said.

Blackie looked up at him and wagged his tail – but he held on to the handle of the basket.

Mandy laughed. 'He isn't getting any more obedient,' she said.

James shoved his hair out of his eyes. 'Down, Blackie!' he said.

Blackie looked up at James sorrowfully and barked. The basket tumbled to the ground.

'Got it,' Mandy said, snatching it up. She looked at Blackie. 'You'll get your share of the picnic, Blackie,' she said.

'Lucky there isn't anything breakable in there,' said Mrs Hope.

Mandy looked at her mum, leaning through the kitchen window of the cottage.

'It's a wonder he could pick it up,' she said. 'What have you put in here, Mum?'

Emily Hope laughed and her green eyes danced. Her red hair shone in the sun. 'Oh, this and that,' she said. 'Enough to keep three hungry people happy.'

'And a hungry dog,' James said, grabbing Blackie's collar before he could get to the basket again.

'Enough for a siege,' said Mr Hope as he got into the car. 'Come on then. We haven't got all day.'

Mrs Hope laughed. 'But that's exactly what you have got,' she said. 'A whole day to ramble on the moors and have a picnic.'

Mandy turned to her mother. 'It's a pity you can't come, Mum,' she said.

Emily Hope shook her head. 'Somebody has to mind the surgery,' she said. 'And it's ages since your dad had a day off.'

'And I'm going to make the most of it,' Adam Hope said. 'Get in, you two – three,' he added, looking at Blackie.

Mandy and James got into the car. Blackie bounded after them.

'Have a good time,' Mrs Hope called.

Jean Knox, the surgery receptionist, appeared at the window beside her. 'Enjoy yourselves,' she said.

Mandy looked back as the car drove out of Animal Ark's driveway. Mrs Hope and Jean waved from the kitchen window. It was a lovely sunny morning and Mandy wished her mum could have come with them. She sighed.

Mr Hope turned his head. 'Someone has to look after the animals,' he said.

Mandy nodded. Animal Ark was a busy veterinary practice and both her parents were vets. They didn't have much free time. And Mum was right: it had been ages since Mr Hope had had a day off.

'It's going to be wonderful,' Mandy said.

Mr Hope laughed. 'That's the spirit!' he said.
'I'm looking forward to this picnic.'

'So is Blackie,' James said.

Mandy gave the Labrador a hug. 'First you have
to do a bit of walking,' Mandy said. 'Then we eat.'

Blackie wagged his tail and knocked James's
glasses off.

'Blackie!' said James, laughing.

Blackie wasn't the most obedient dog in
the world – or the best behaved – but he was
great fun.

'Where are we going?' James said as he settled
his glasses back on his nose.

Mandy turned round to point out of the car
window to the moor above Welford village. 'Up
there,' she said. 'Black Tor.'

'Terrific,' said James. 'It's ages since I've been
up to Black Tor.'

The car swung round the crossroads by the
Fox and Goose pub and Mandy and James waved
to Mr Hardy, the publican, as they passed. He
looked up from rolling a barrel into the pub and
waved back.

Then they were out of the village and climbing
towards the moor. Mandy loved the moor. It could

be wild and windy in winter and the snow could pile itself into drifts two metres deep. But today, in the spring sunshine, it looked perfect.

The car climbed higher and Mandy and James looked back. Welford lay spread out below them. They could see Animal Ark, the old stone cottage at the front and the modern extension that housed the surgery at the back. They spotted James's house at the other end of the village and Mandy's grandparents' cottage with their camper van sitting outside. And behind the Fox and Goose was the lane where Walter Pickard and Ernie Bell lived, both church bell-ringers like Grandad. Then there was the church and the post office and the village hall.

'It looks like a toy village,' James said.

'Look,' said Mandy. 'You can see Walton. There's the school.' Walton was the neighbouring town, two miles from Welford.

'Ugh!' groaned James. 'Don't mention school. Not when the holidays have just begun!'

'And there's the cottage hospital,' Mandy said, pointing to a long, low building on the outskirts of Walton. It was the little local hospital for Walton and Welford. 'Gran says there's a new matron there now.'

James nodded. 'I know,' he said. 'Johnny Pearson broke his leg playing football. He's in the cottage hospital. Mark says he's scared stiff of Matron.' Mark was Johnny's older brother. He was in Mandy's class at school.

Mandy pulled a face. 'She must be bad if Johnny's scared of her,' she said. 'Johnny's a holy terror.'

James grinned. 'Mark says it's time somebody kept Johnny in line.'

Mandy turned to face the way they were going. 'Look, Dad,' she said. 'There are lambs in the fields already.'

Mr Hope's beard twitched as he smiled. 'As if I didn't know it,' he said. 'How many call-outs did I have last week?'

'Ooops, sorry!' Mandy said. The Hopes were always very busy at lambing time.

James was looking out of the side window. 'Mrs McFarlane was saying that somebody has moved into Fordbeck Farm,' he said.

The McFarlanes ran the Welford post office. Mrs McFarlane knew everything that was going on almost before it happened.

Mr Hope nodded. 'The Spillers,' he said. 'I've been in to see them a couple of times.'

'The people with the little girl?' said Mandy.

Her dad nodded. 'Jenny. She's six. And Mrs Spiller is expecting another baby any day now.'

'Have they got lambs?' Mandy said.

Mr Hope nodded again. 'This is their first lambing season. The Spillers aren't country folk. Mr Spiller lost his job and they bought that old farm. I have to hand it to Jack Spiller. He's making a good job of it. Only thing is, they can't afford to pay anybody to help them so he's having to do it all himself.'

Mandy opened her mouth to ask why Mrs Spiller didn't help. She was so used to her mum and dad working together, sharing the load. Then she remembered about the new baby.

'That must be hard at lambing time,' James said.

Mr Hope gave him a smile. 'That's why I thought you wouldn't mind if we popped in on the way to Black Tor. Just to see how they're getting on.'

Mandy grinned. Typical. If her dad thought someone needed a hand he would be there – day off or no day off.

'I'd love to see some lambs,' Mandy said.

Mr Hope glanced at Blackie but James said 'No need to worry. Blackie's no bother around sheep. He's as gentle as . . .'

'A lamb,' Mandy finished and they laughed.

'In here then,' Mr Hope said and he swung the car down a dirt track off the road.

The track was bumpy – as if it hadn't been used in a long time.

'How long have they been here?' James asked.

Mr Hope shrugged. 'About eight months,' he said. 'Jack Spiller has worked his socks off on that farm, trying to make a go of it.'

'It was pretty run down, wasn't it?' James said.

Mr Hope nodded. 'That's the only reason he could afford it. He's put every penny he has into it. And done the work on the farm buildings himself. But you don't get too much done in winter. Let's hope things start looking up for them soon.'

Mandy looked at her dad thoughtfully. It sounded as if the Spillers were having a hard time.

The car bumped and jolted its way along the track and turned in at the farmyard.

Mandy looked round. The farmhouse was the long, low, old-fashioned kind. But it had been freshly whitewashed and there were daffodils growing in half barrels at the door and pots of geraniums on the window ledge. The curtains at the windows were blue gingham and the whole place looked neat and clean.

'Needs some work doing on that barn,' Mr Hope said as he stopped the car.

Mandy looked at the barn. It was true. It did look a bit run down, but there was fresh wood showing here and there where it had been mended. It was clear Mr Spiller was working on the place.

'He's started mending it,' she said. Then she saw an old shed in the far corner of the farmyard. 'Look at that,' she said.

Mr Hope looked. 'That's beyond mending,' he said. 'That needs to be knocked down.'

Mr Hope tooted the horn. Nothing. No sign of life.

Mandy looked at the blue curtains blowing at the windows of the house. Where were the Spillers?

'Jack Spiller is probably out lambing,' said Mr Hope.

'What about Mrs Spiller and the little girl?' Mandy said.

Mr Hope shook his head. He looked worried.

'Maybe you should go inside,' James said to him. 'The door is open.'

Mr Hope hesitated. He wasn't the type to go barging into people's houses without asking. But

Mandy could see he was concerned.

Just then a little girl emerged from the house. Her dark hair was tied in bunches with bright red ribbons. The ribbons matched her red jumper and red gumboots. She stood on the doorstep looking at them.

'Look,' said Mandy.

'That's Jenny,' Mr Hope said.

Mandy scrambled out of the car and walked slowly across the farmyard. The little girl looked scared to death. Mandy didn't want to frighten her any more.

'Hello,' she said as she got nearer. 'You're Jenny, aren't you?'

The child nodded, but didn't say a word.

Mandy smiled encouragingly. 'Where's your mum?' she said.

Jenny turned her face up to Mandy and her eyes filled with tears. She raised a hand and pointed into the house. 'In there,' she said. 'She's sick. She's got a sore tummy – and Daddy isn't here.'

James and Mr Hope were out of the car now.

'Dad?' said Mandy.

Mr Hope's face looked worried. 'I heard,' he said quietly. 'Keep Jenny out here while I go and see what's wrong.'

And he strode into the house.

Mandy and James looked at each other. Jenny's face was streaming with tears now. Mandy reached an arm out to give her a hug but then Blackie bounded up and began to lick the little girl's face.

It was like magic. At once the tears disappeared.

'Oh!' said Jenny. 'Is he yours?'

'He's mine,' James said. 'His name is Blackie.'

Jenny put her hand out to stroke the Labrador. 'He's lovely,' she said. 'Can I play with him? Daddy doesn't let me play with Jess.'

'Of course you can play with him,' James said. Then he turned to Mandy. 'Who's Jess?' he said.

Mandy shrugged her shoulders. Things at Fordbeck Farm were getting stranger and stranger.

It seemed like ages but it could only have been minutes before Mr Hope came out of the house. His face looked very serious.

He drew Mandy away from Jenny and spoke in a low voice.

'Mrs Spiller's baby is on the way, Mandy,' he said. 'I don't think we have much time.'

'She isn't going to have it here, is she?' said Mandy.

Mr Hope shook his head. 'I don't think that would be a good idea,' he said. 'Lambing is one thing but human babies are another.'

Mandy looked at Jenny playing happily with Blackie and James. James was doing a great job keeping the little girl's mind off her mother.

'Is there anything I can do?' Mandy said.

Mr Hope nodded. 'I can't leave Mrs Spiller – just in case,' he said. 'Jack Spiller is in the top field, lambing. Go and fetch him.'

Mandy's mind teemed with questions but one look at her dad's face told her there was no time.

'Tell him to get back here right now,' said Mr Hope. 'He's got to get his wife to the cottage hospital.'

Mandy stood stock-still for a moment, looking at her dad. It wasn't often he was so abrupt. He looked really worried.

'Run!' her dad said.

Mandy turned on her heels and ran for the top field.

Two

Mandy ran like she had never run before. It *would* be the top field, she thought. The one furthest away from the farmhouse. Her breath rasping in her throat, she scrambled over a dry-stone wall and raced over the field. She looked up. There, outlined against the sky, she could see the figure of a man. He was bending over a sheep. It had to be Jack Spiller.

'Mr Spiller!' she shouted.

But the wind whipped her voice away. Panting, Mandy raced on. 'Mr Spiller!' she called again as she drew nearer.

The tall, dark-haired figure straightened up

and turned round. A flowing black and white shape rose up from the grass and streaked towards her.

'Jess!' Mr Spiller cried and at once the shape halted and turned. Jess was a sheepdog.

Mandy stumbled the last few metres and stood looking up at the farmer, out of breath.

'Mr Spiller,' she said again.

He was a tall man with a kind face and worried eyes. He looked down at her, puzzled.

'That's me,' he said. 'Who are you?'

'Mandy Hope,' Mandy said.

The man's face cleared. 'The vet's daughter?' he said and smiled.

Mandy nodded. Her breath was coming back now. She reached out a hand and tugged at Jack Spiller's sleeve.

'You've got to come,' she said. 'Back to the farm. It's your wife . . .'

At once his smile disappeared. 'Maggie?' he said. 'What's wrong? Has she had an accident?'

Mandy shook her head. 'No,' she said. 'But the baby is coming. Dad says she needs to go to the cottage hospital – right away.'

The words were hardly out of her mouth before Jack Spiller was off, racing down the field, leaping

the dry-stone wall as if it was nothing, running for home with Jess beside him.

Mandy watched as he crossed the bottom field. She hoped Mrs Spiller would be all right – and the baby.

She felt something soft and warm nudge her leg and looked down. A lamb, hardly a day old, blundered into her. Mandy smiled in spite of her worry. It looked so small and fluffy. A ewe, its mother, bleated to it and the lamb turned and trotted towards her. The ewe gave it a gentle butt with its head and the lamb drew close to its mother's side, nuzzling for milk.

Mandy gave herself a shake. The lamb was beautiful but this was no time to stand there admiring it. She turned and ran back down the hill towards the farm.

Mr Hope was helping a young woman into a dilapidated old van when Mandy arrived at the farmyard. Jess, the sheepdog, crouched watchfully beside the farmhouse door.

'Well done, Mandy,' her dad said.

Mandy glowed with pleasure and looked at the woman. She had short dark hair and cheeks that should have been rosy. But now she looked pale and drawn. She turned a worried face to Mandy.

'Thank you so much,' she said. Then she looked at Mr Hope as she eased herself into the van. 'But what about Jenny?'

Mr Hope looked at Mandy and James. Jenny was absorbed in talking to Blackie, kneeling beside him.

'We'll look after her,' Mandy said. 'Won't we, James?'

James smiled. 'Of course we will,' he said. 'Blackie will help.'

Mandy saw some of the worry fade from Mrs Spiller's face.

Then Jack Spiller came hurtling out of the house with a bag overflowing with clothes.

Mrs Spiller smiled. 'I wasn't quite packed,' she said. 'The baby is a bit early.'

Mr Spiller threw the bag into the back of the van. Then he turned to look at Jenny.

'Don't worry about her,' Mr Hope said. 'We'll look after Jenny.'

Mr Spiller ran a hand through his hair. 'I don't like asking favours,' he said.

Mr Hope smiled. 'It isn't a favour,' he said. 'It's a pleasure. Anyway, we have to give one another a hand here in the country.'

Mr Spiller looked at him gratefully. 'I'll be back

as soon as I can,' he said. He looked at his wife and she smiled at him.

'I'll be all right,' she said. 'Just drop me at the hospital.' She turned to Mr Hope. 'It's the lambing, you see,' she said. 'We can't afford to get anybody to help us and I haven't been able to do much to help Jack recently. He just can't be away from the farm for very long.'

Jack Spiller's mouth looked grim. 'You've probably helped too much,' he said to his wife. 'I shouldn't have let you.'

'Don't be daft,' Mrs Spiller said. 'You can't manage it all on your own.'

'I'll have to,' said Jack Spiller. He turned and looked towards the top field. 'There are one or two ewes I'm not happy about up there,' he said. Then he gave Jess the order to stay and got into the van beside his wife.

James came and stood beside Mandy. 'He can't do all that lambing on his own,' he said softly.

Mandy nodded thoughtfully. 'And he really should be with Mrs Spiller at the hospital.'

'What do you think?' said James.

Mandy looked at him. 'No picnic?' she said.

James shrugged. 'I don't mind. There are plenty of days for a picnic.'

'Not for Dad,' Mandy said. 'He hasn't had a day off in ages.'

'He wouldn't mind,' said James.

Mandy grinned. 'No, I don't suppose he would,' she said.

The van engine was revving up. Jenny looked up and ran to the passenger side.

'Will you bring a baby home, Mummy?' she said.

Mrs Spiller smiled but Mandy saw a spasm of pain cross her face. 'In a few days,' she said. 'Be a good girl for Daddy while I'm away.'

The little girl nodded. 'I'll help him,' she said. 'With the lambs.'

'So will we,' Mandy said impulsively. She turned to her father. 'Won't we, Dad?'

Mr Hope smiled. 'Of course we will,' he said. 'I've got gumboots in the car for everybody.'

Jack Spiller's face lit up. 'Really?' he said. 'You'll stay?'

'Take your time,' Mr Hope said. 'We'll look after the lambing for you – Mandy and James and I.'

'And me!' said little Jenny.

Mr Hope laughed. 'And you,' he said.

'I don't know what to say,' Jack Spiller said. 'I never expected kindness like this. You'll find the lambing bag in the top field – I hope the ewes haven't got at it.'

Mr Hope looked at Mrs Spiller. Her face was very pale. 'Don't worry about that,' he said. 'Just get going!'

The engine revved again. Mr Spiller waved and the van was off.

'What's a lambing bag?' said James.

Mr Hope laughed. 'It's the most important thing a shepherd or a sheep farmer has at lambing time,' he said. 'I'll show it to you when we find it.'

'Right,' said Mandy as they watched the van disappear round a bend in the track. 'Let's get to work then.'

'The top field, Jack said,' Mr Hope said. 'I think we'd better take a look up there first.'

'Shall we take Jess?' Mandy said.

Mr Hope nodded. 'We'll need her,' he said. 'Sometimes ewes can bolt and you need a sheepdog to catch them.'

Mr Hope whistled to the black and white collie which came running to his heels. 'Lucky Jess and I have met before,' he said. 'She's a good sheepdog.'

'What about Blackie?' James said.

Mr Hope looked at the Labrador. 'Better put

him on the lead,' he said. 'I know he wouldn't harm the sheep but the sheep don't know that. A ewe panics easily at this time of year.'

Jenny looked up from where she was cuddling Blackie. 'Can I take him?' she said.

James smiled. 'Of course you can,' he said as he clipped on Blackie's lead.

They got gumboots and Mr Hope's bag from the car, then the procession started up towards the top field. Mr Hope with Jess, Mandy and James and Jenny with Blackie.

So much for Dad's day off, Mandy thought.

As they went Mr Hope explained what needed to be done.

'We spread out,' he said. 'We have to check on as many ewes as possible, looking for signs of distress.'

'What signs?' James said.

Mr Hope thought for a moment. 'If you see a ewe lying down, she's probably lambing. But ewes are strange creatures. They're just as likely to give birth standing up as lying down. In any case, you must keep watch to see that the lamb is born safely. Once the birth process starts it doesn't take too long.'

'How do you know everything is OK?' Mandy said.

Mr Hope smiled. 'You'll see the lamb born, then the ewe will get to her feet and start licking the lamb. Once that happens you can be sure everything will be all right.'

'What if the ewe doesn't lick the lamb?' James said.

Mr Hope frowned. 'That can be difficult,' he said. 'You see, if the bond between mother and child isn't formed at once, you can find yourself with a rejected lamb on your hands – and a lot more work. Either you have to bring the rejected lambs into the house and hand rear them or you have to set them on to another ewe.'

'Huh?' said James.

Mr Hope smiled. 'Setting on is when you take the skin of a dead lamb, maybe one that was stillborn, and put it on a rejected lamb. Then, if you're lucky, the mother will think it's her own lamb and feed it.'

'I suppose that's better than having to hand rear a whole lot of lambs,' James said, but he didn't sound too keen on the idea of setting on.

'It's certainly less work,' said Mr Hope.

'And Mr Spiller is so busy already,' James said.

'He wouldn't have time for hand rearing. Lambs have to be fed so often when they're really young.'

Mr Hope smiled at him. 'Sheep farmers don't get much time to rest during lambing. Ask any of them. And besides, it's the farmers' wives that usually do the hand rearing – in the kitchen. Now spread out,' he said. 'The first thing we have to do is find the lambing bag.'

They spread out. Mandy was so enchanted with the little woolly lambs that skipped and hopped beside their mothers that she almost forgot what she was supposed to be looking for. It was James who shouted 'Is this it?'

Mandy looked round. James was holding up a dun-coloured bag with a cord attached.

'That's it,' said Mr Hope, coming over to him. 'Now you can see what's in a lambing bag.'

Mr Hope took the bag and opened it. Mandy and James and Jenny looked on as he emptied it.

'It's a sort of survival kit for sheep farmers,' he said as he laid the various things out on the grass. 'You see, there's string and marking fluid for identifying lambs. Then there's penicillin for giving before a difficult birth. There's lambing oil for when the farmer has to help the birth along and protein drinks for exhaustion, calcium and a

mixture for enteritis. Then the whole bag is lined with sheep's-wool so that if you have to bring a lamb home it'll be cosy and warm in there.'

'That's marvellous,' said Mandy.

Mr Hope nodded. 'Oh, lambing bags are great things,' he said. 'Now, let's get to work.'

They worked hard until midday, when Mr Hope said they could stop and eat their picnic.

'No problems to report?' Mr Hope said as they settled themselves behind a dry-stone wall.

Mandy shook her head, her cheeks aglow as she spread the picnic on the grass beside them. There were pasties and crusty rolls and shiny red apples and wedges of cheese. And there were slabs of fruit cake and tubs of yoghurt to finish with.

'Oh, Dad, I saw a lamb being born! And it was just like you said,' Mandy said.

'I saw one as well,' James said. 'It was tiny. It got up right away and its mother did just what you said – started licking it. Then it began to feed.'

Mr Hope laughed. 'I'm glad you're enjoying it,' he said.

Mandy munched on a vegetable pasty. 'This is good,' she said.

'Hard work makes for good appetites,' Mr Hope said.

James nodded. 'It's good to sit down,' he said.

Jenny looked up, her mouth full of crusty roll and cheese. 'Can I give some to Blackie?' she said.

James nodded and the little girl smiled.

'You really like Blackie, don't you?' he said.

Jenny nodded. 'Dad won't let me play with Jess,' she said. 'I like playing with Blackie. I'd like my own Blackie.'

'Work dogs aren't for playing with,' said Mr Hope. He looked round. 'Where is Jess, anyway?'

Just at that moment a black and white shape raced over the hill and stood a few metres away, looking at them.

'Here, girl,' said Mandy but the dog stood its ground. Her head moved slightly back and forth.

At once Mr Hope was on the alert. He stood up and the sheepdog started to move away.

'What is it, Dad?' Mandy said.

Mr Hope took a step forward. Jess looked back towards him and moved a further few metres.

'I think Jess is trying to tell us something,' Mr Hope said.

Mandy scrambled to her feet. 'What?' she said.

Mr Hope shook his head. 'I don't know,' he said, 'but I think we'd better find out!'

Three

Jess loped in front of them, looking back now and then to see that they were following.

'She's trying to tell us something,' Mandy said.

James nodded. 'It looks like it.'

Mr Hope pointed. 'There,' he said. 'Just under the dry-stone wall.'

Mandy and James looked. A ewe lay stretched out on the ground. As they got closer Mandy could see more clearly. The ewe wasn't moving. She was lying flat on her side, her legs stiff, her body arched.

'Is she dead?' Mandy said.

Mr Hope was already opening the lambing bag.

'No,' he said, 'but there isn't much time.'

'She isn't moving,' said James, 'and her eyes are closed.'

As if the ewe had heard, she opened her eyes and gave a weak bleat.

'Careful now,' said Mr Hope. 'We don't want to alarm her.'

'What's wrong, Dad?' said Mandy.

Mr Hope bent to the ewe and ran his hands over her stiff body.

'Hypocalcaemia,' he said shortly.

'What's that?' said Mandy, kneeling beside him. 'Can you do something for her?'

Mr Hope searched in the lambing bag. 'It's a deficiency of calcium,' he said. 'It sometimes happens with pregnant ewes.'

'Can you cure it?' James asked.

Mr Hope nodded. 'I hope so,' he said. 'If it isn't too late.'

Mandy saw her dad take a syringe out of the bag and a plastic bottle filled with some kind of solution.

'I have to give her an injection,' he said. 'We must just hope it's in time. Mandy, hold her head while I do it.'

Mandy put her arms round the ewe's head. It felt heavy and the ewe was hardly breathing. 'Quick,

Dad,' she said. 'I think she's in real trouble!'

Swiftly, Mr Hope filled the syringe and injected the ewe.

'What now?' said James.

'Now we wait,' said Mr Hope.

'How long?' said Mandy.

Mr Hope smiled. 'Not long,' he said. 'If it works.'

They stood there watching the ewe as the minutes ticked by. Mandy held her breath. She thought she saw the ewe's eyes flicker. Then a tremor ran through the ewe's body and her eyes opened. The frightened animal looked up at Mandy and bleated pitifully.

'Dad?' Mandy said.

Her dad nodded. 'I felt it,' he said. He turned to James. 'Help Mandy hold her head,' he said, 'and get ready to hold the ewe in case she bolts. I rather think I'm going to be busy at this end.'

'Bolts?' said James as he went to help Mandy.

Mr Hope nodded. 'Ewes in trouble often bolt. And with this one so close to giving birth that wouldn't be a good idea.'

Mandy's eyes opened wide. 'Is the lamb coming?' she said.

Mr Hope nodded. 'Soon,' he said. 'But I think she'll need some help.'

Mandy opened her mouth to ask more questions but at that moment the ewe gave a shudder and began to struggle to her feet.

Mandy and James locked their arms round the ewe's neck as she stood shaking her head and pawing at the short grass. Then she gave a long bleat and strained against them.

'Hold her,' Mr Hope said urgently.

Mandy tightened her grip, talking to the frightened animal, soothing her. The ewe began to calm down.

Mandy looked at her father. He rolled his sleeves up and quickly rubbed some lambing oil on his hands and forearms. He looked up briefly.

'Hold tight,' he said. 'Here we go.'

Mandy watched as her father felt for the little creature. She saw him frown.

'What is it, Dad?'

'Twins,' he said. 'And they're a bit mixed up in there.'

Mandy bit her lip. The poor ewe's body heaved with effort and her eyes rolled upwards.

'It'll all be over soon,' Mandy said to her.

Another long shudder passed through the ewe's body. Mandy looked at her dad's face. He was intent on what he was doing. Then she saw him grin.

'Come on, little fellow,' he said. 'There's another one behind you.'

And suddenly her dad's hands were full of newborn lamb as it slipped and slid on the grass. Swiftly he guided the shaking little creature round to its mother's side.

'For goodness sake, don't let her go now,' he said to Mandy and James. 'There's another lamb to come and if she doesn't start licking them right away, we'll have two rejected lambs.'

Mandy shifted her grasp so that the ewe could get to her lamb. She watched, breathless, as the ewe started licking the little creature clean.

'It's so tiny,' she said, looking at the lamb as its mother cleaned it up.

'And here's another,' Mr Hope said, coming to stand beside her.

Mandy looked up. She had been so busy watching the first lamb she had missed the birth of the second.

'Oh, Dad,' she said as Mr Hope put the second lamb down and the ewe began to clean that one too. 'Two lambs – and the poor ewe looked so sick!'

James grinned. 'Your dad can cure anything,' he said.

Mr Hope laughed. 'Hypocalcaemia isn't hard

to cure if you have the right treatment. But it's Jess we have to thank. If she hadn't come to fetch us the ewe would never have made it.'

'And those two little lambs would have died too,' Mandy said. 'What a good dog you are, Jess!'

She turned to give Jess a hug but Jess was looking away down the hill. Her ears were cocked. She was on the alert.

'What is it, girl?' said Mandy. 'Another ewe in trouble?'

But Jess was off, running down the hill towards the farm, long strides covering the distance fast.

Jenny jumped up and down. 'It's Daddy!' she said. 'Jess always does that when Daddy comes home.'

And Jenny was off after Jess.

'Mrs Spiller and the baby,' Mandy said. 'I'd almost forgotten about them.'

'Look!' said James.

He was pointing to a tall figure striding up the hill from the farm. Jack Spiller. As they watched, they saw Jess reach him. Mr Spiller bent down and gave her a pat. Then he saw Jenny running towards him.

Her voice carried on the wind. 'Daddy, Daddy, have we got a baby?'

Jack Spiller broke into a run and gathered

his daughter up in his arms, lifting her high over his head.

Mandy felt herself smiling as he swung the little girl up on his shoulders and walked towards them, the dog at his heels.

'A boy!' he shouted as he drew near. 'A beautiful baby boy and Maggie is just fine. Exhausted but fine.'

Mandy grinned and looked at the twin lambs, now busy suckling. Their white woolly coats had dried in the breeze. They looked as if they were made out of fluffy cotton wool. Their little tails wagged madly as they fed.

'I'll bet the new baby is just as beautiful as you,' Mandy said softly to the lambs.

Four

'Home!' said Mandy as the car turned down the track to Animal Ark.

'I'm exhausted,' said James.

Mr Hope laughed. 'Lambing is hard work,' he said.

Mandy frowned. 'Too hard for one person. Too hard for Mr Spiller all on his own – especially with Jenny to look after while Mrs Spiller is in hospital.'

Mr Hope drove through the gate of Animal Ark, past the wooden sign swinging gently in the breeze. Mr Hope drew the car to a standstill and turned to them. 'You know, you could help him,' he said. 'You were a terrific help to me today.'

Mandy shook her short, fair hair out of her eyes. 'Us?' she said. 'But we don't know the first thing about lambing.'

'We might do something wrong,' said James.

Mr Hope shrugged. 'Just a thought,' he said. 'But Jack can't be everywhere at once and he certainly can't afford to lose too many lambs. It's a matter of having somebody there to deal with trouble before it happens – like you were doing for me today.'

'You mean like Jess and that ewe?' said James.

Mr Hope nodded. 'That's what I mean. That ewe was ready to bolt. If it hadn't been for you two holding on to her we might have lost the lambs.' He smiled. 'Think about it,' he said.

Mandy's eyes were shining. 'We don't have to think about it, do we, James?' she said. 'Of course we'll help Mr Spiller – if he'll let us!'

Mr Hope laughed. 'Oh, I think he'll let you all right. Jack Spiller's got too much on his plate to refuse an offer of help right now.'

Mandy smiled up at her dad. He really was kind. If Mr Spiller needed help, then Mr Spiller would get help.

'The only thing is . . .' said Mr Hope.

James and Mandy looked at him. Mr Hope scratched his ear uncomfortably.

'What is it?' said Mandy.

'Jack Spiller came here knowing hardly anything about sheep,' Mr Hope said. 'And he's made a good job of things so far – without asking for help.'

Mandy began to see what her dad was driving at.

'Oh, Dad, we won't go charging in saying that you've been telling us he's in trouble.'

'No, I know you won't,' said Mr Hope. 'It's just that he has his pride and he's done a good job already.'

'I know,' said James. 'We'll ask him if he'd take us on for training, sort of – if it wouldn't be too much trouble. How about that?'

'Then we can help him while he thinks he's helping us,' said Mandy. 'Brilliant! James, you're a genius.'

James flushed with pleasure and shoved his glasses up his nose.

Mr Hope looked at them both. 'James might be a genius,' he said, 'but I'm starving. How about you?'

'Tea,' said Mandy. 'My stomach feels like a great big empty cave.'

'Come on, James,' said Mr Hope. 'Ring your mum and tell her you're eating with us tonight.'

Blackie gave a bark. 'And you too, Blackie.' Mr Hope laughed. 'Would I forget you?'

Mrs Hope and Gran were sitting in the sunny kitchen of Animal Ark. A pot of tea stood on the table between them.

Emily Hope put down her teacup and looked at them in amazement. 'Where on earth have you three been?' she said.

'Had a good picnic?' said Gran at the same time.

Mandy looked down at her muddy clothes and even muddier gumboots. Then she looked at Mr Hope and James. They weren't any better.

Mr Hope ran a hand through his hair. 'You don't stay clean chasing sheep,' he said.

'Sheep?' said Emily Hope.

'On a picnic?' Gran said to her son. Adam Hope might be a grown-up vet to the rest of Welford but to Gran he was still her boy – and a very muddy one at the moment.

'Tell you what,' said Mr Hope, sidling out of the kitchen. 'Why don't we get cleaned up, then we can tell you all about it over tea.'

Gran looked at her watch. 'Goodness! Is that the time already?' she said. 'I must get home.' She bustled about, picking up her coat and giving Emily Hope a hug.

She turned to Mandy and stopped. Mandy grinned. 'It's all right, Gran,' she said. 'I'm much to muddy to hug. I'll save it for next time.'

'Mmm,' said Gran. 'Maybe you're right.' She put on her coat. 'Tell you what,' she said. 'Come round tomorrow, you and James. There's something I want you to help me with.'

'What?' said Mandy.

Gran's eyes twinkled. 'I'm on the campaigning trail again,' she said.

'Not the post office,' said Mandy. 'You won that campaign.'

Gran had organised a campaign to save the McFarlanes' little office in the village when it had been threatened with closure.

'No,' said Gran. 'They're leaving the post office alone. It's the cottage hospital they want to close now.'

Mandy's jaw dropped. 'What?' she said. 'But they can't do that!'

Gran nodded grimly. 'They can if they want,' she said. 'But I intend to make them change their minds.'

'How?' said Mandy.

Gran thought for a moment. 'I don't know exactly,' she admitted. 'We'll need a plan. But one thing's for sure, by the time we're finished, I want them to regret the day they ever thought of closing the cottage hospital! So, can I count you in?' She looked from Mandy to James.

'Of course you can,' said James. 'I remember having my tonsils out there. It's a great place. They gave me ice-cream. And it's so close to school that everybody could come to visit me on their way home. I really enjoyed it.'

Mandy thought of the little cottage hospital near their school in Walton. It was as pretty as a picture with a flower garden in front and green painted shutters on the windows. 'What does Matron say?' she asked.

Gran's eyes twinkled even more as she buttoned up her coat. 'Matron,' she said, 'is on the warpath.'

Mandy felt herself grinning. 'Johnny Pearson is terrified of her,' she said.

Gran laughed. 'Matron's bark is a lot worse that her bite,' she said.

'Even when she's on the warpath?' said James.

Gran laughed again. 'Don't worry, James,' she said. 'I'm the one you'll be helping.' She picked

up her bag. 'Right,' she said. 'I'm off. I'll see you two tomorrow morning.'

'Bye, Gran,' said Mandy and turned to her mother, full of news of Mrs Spiller's baby and questions about the hospital.

Mrs Hope shook her head. 'Oh, no,' she said. 'Not until you clean yourselves up. Wash first, talk later!'

Mandy, James and Mr Hope filed out. Blackie tried to follow them but Mrs Hope stopped him. 'Oh, no, you don't,' she said. 'I'm going to give you a good brushing, Blackie.'

Blackie looked resigned. With Emily Hope

in this mood it was no good anyone arguing with her.

'That was wonderful,' James sighed, leaning back in his chair. 'Thanks, Mrs Hope.'

Mrs Hope smiled at him. 'Glad you enjoyed it, James,' she said, looking at the empty plates on the table.

Mandy followed her eyes and laughed. 'We were hungry, Mum,' she said. 'Besides, it really was an excellent tea.'

They'd eaten quiche and salad and baked potatoes with cheese and coleslaw fillings, followed by the big floury scones Gran had brought, topped with butter and Mrs Hope's home-made strawberry jam. Mandy felt as if she would never move again – and said so.

Mr Hope laughed. 'And who's going to help your poor old father with the animals tonight?' he said.

'You know I wouldn't miss that, Dad,' Mandy said. 'I love helping in the surgery – but maybe not straight away.'

'I should think not,' said Mrs Hope. 'You ate like a horse, Mandy.' She looked at her daughter, slim and long-legged. 'I honestly don't know where you put it!' she said. She leaned her elbows on the table. 'It will really please Gran if you help her with this campaign.'

Mandy looked indignant. 'Of course we'll help her. I mean, how can they think of closing the cottage hospital?'

'To save money,' Mr Hope said.

Mandy shook her head. 'And what about the people who live here – what about Mrs Spiller?' she said.

'That's true,' said Mrs Hope. 'From what your dad says, Mrs Spiller got to the hospital just in time. That little baby was in quite a hurry to be born.'

Adam Hope nodded in agreement. 'And there's the visiting,' he said. 'Jack Spiller would never manage to visit every day if they were much further away – not at lambing time.'

Emily Hope nodded. 'That's a good angle to take for your campaign, Mandy,' she said. 'It isn't just a hospital – it's a life-line in a place like this.'

James grinned. 'And that's a good slogan,' he said. '"It isn't just a hospital – it's a life-line." Do you think your Gran will want to do posters?' he said.

Mandy laughed. 'You know Gran, she'll want to

do everything,' she said. 'Come on, let's take care of the animals and talk about it.'

'OK,' said James, getting up from the table.

'We'll make a start on the cages, Dad,' said Mandy.

'All right,' said Mr Hope. 'I'll be there in a few minutes to do the dressings and medications.'

'Oh,' said Mrs Hope, 'that reminds me. Tom is in again. And he isn't too happy about the dressing I put on him this afternoon.'

'Tom?' said Mandy. 'Again? What happened this time?'

Mrs Hope smiled. 'He took on a terrier twice his size – and he got the worst of it. Five stitches. And stitching Tom up is not my favourite job.'

Mandy shook her head. Tom was Walter Pickard's big black and white cat. He was a real gangster of the cat world, always in trouble.

'So what's the plan?' said James as they made their way into the residential unit.

Mandy looked around the unit. There weren't too many animals in at the moment. A puppy with an infected ear, a gerbil with an eye infection, a tortoise with a rather serious cyst, and Tom. Mandy looked at him, crouched like a sleeping lion in his cage.

'I reckon we should do a poster campaign. Then maybe a petition.'

'And try to get the *Walton Gazette* involved,' said James.

'Good idea,' Mandy said. 'We might even try to get one of the big papers in York interested.'

'Steady,' Mandy said as James approached Tom's cage. 'You undo the latch while I try to charm him out of there.'

Tom lifted his great black and white head and regarded them lazily. The black patch over one eye made him look like a pirate.

'OK, then, Tom,' James said to him. 'No need to get annoyed. We just want to clean your cage out, that's all.'

Tom's massive head swung to look at James and his yellow eyes focused. Then, very slowly, he gathered himself up on to his haunches and spat.

'Oh, Tom,' said Mandy. 'We're only trying to help.' She looked at the dressing on the back of his neck. It was pretty thickly wadded. He must have got a bad bite from that dog. 'Oh, Tom,' she said again, 'why do you get yourself into trouble all the time?'

'That's a question we all ask ourselves,' said Mr Hope, coming into the residential unit. He smiled at Mandy and James. 'That cage looks pretty clean to me,' he said. 'Why don't you leave it until tomorrow? Maybe Tom will be feeling a bit better by then.'

Mandy grinned. 'You think so?' she said.

Mr Hope laughed. 'No, I don't,' he said. 'But you look dead on your feet. Time you were off to bed. And James's mum will think he's lost.'

'I'm pretty tired too,' said James. 'An early night isn't a bad idea.'

Mandy gave an enormous yawn. Tom opened his huge jaws and did the same.

'Good night, Tom,' Mandy said. 'Sleep well.'

Tom gave her a dismissive look and, turning his back on all of them, curled up and went to sleep.

Five

For the next week Mandy didn't know whether she was on her head or her heels. When they weren't at Lilac Cottage doing posters and leaflets for Gran, they were at Fordbeck Farm helping Mr Spiller.

By the end of the week Mandy had designed a dozen posters with the life-line slogan and she also felt she knew nearly everything there was to know about lambing. The weather had been really good and Jack Spiller was pleased with the crop of little lambs. None of the new lambs had to be brought into the kitchen and the ones that Mrs Spiller had been hand rearing were almost ready to be put out in the field.

'I really appreciate your help,' Mr Spiller said to Mandy and James as they stood in the top field watching several woolly lambs frisking round their mothers.

'We haven't done much,' said James.

Jack Spiller laughed. 'You've done enough,' he said. 'Keeping an eye out and letting me know at any sign of trouble, catching the ewes when they bolt, fetching the extra feed. Even helping with the hand rearing. It all helps.'

Mandy and James flushed with pleasure.

'We've enjoyed it,' Mandy said.

'Especially chasing the bolting ewes,' James said. 'Why do they do that?'

Jack Spiller shook his head. 'I think they get frightened,' he said. 'But one thing is sure, it's a lot harder to catch a bolting ewe on your own!'

They all laughed. It was a wonderful spring morning. A light breeze stirred Mandy's hair against her cheek. The sky was blue and the sun shone.

'It's a lovely day for Mrs Spiller coming home,' she said.

Jack Spiller's face split into a wide grin. 'It certainly is,' he said. 'And I'll be glad to have them back – both of them.' His grin got even wider.

'Have you decided what to call the baby?' Mandy said.

Mr Spiller looked a bit shy all of a sudden. 'We thought Adam,' he said. 'After your dad. If it hadn't been for him arriving to see if he could help that day . . .' He didn't finish.

Mandy tried to imagine what would have happened if they hadn't stopped by on their way to their picnic. Would Mrs Spiller have been all right?

'I think that's wonderful,' Mandy said. 'Dad will be so pleased.'

Jack Spiller's face looked relieved. 'You don't think he'll mind?'

'Mind?' said Mandy. 'He'll be like a dog with two tails. Just you wait and see.'

Jack Spiller grinned again. He looked quite young when he wasn't looking worried. 'If it had been a girl we'd have called her Mandy,' he said.

Mandy felt herself flush with pleasure. 'A boy is nice,' she said, embarrassed. 'You've got a girl already.'

At that Jack Spiller looked down towards the farmyard where Jenny was playing with Blackie. 'She just loves that dog,' he said.

'And Blackie has a great time with her,' said James. 'She really looks after him well and it means we don't have to tie him up.'

Mandy looked at her watch. 'Mr Spiller,' she said, 'what time did you say you were collecting Mrs Spiller and the baby?'

Jack Spiller looked at his own watch. 'Oh, Lord,' he said. 'I'll have to run. You're sure you'll be all right while I'm gone?'

Mandy smiled. 'Of course we will,' she said. 'We'll have the kettle on for a cup of tea for Mrs Spiller when you get back.'

They watched as Jack Spiller strode off down the field and into the farmyard. He scooped up his daughter and they saw him get into the van and start off down the track.

'Adam,' Mandy said. 'Isn't that nice?'

James grinned. 'Come on,' he said. 'We've got work to do!' And he whistled to Jess to come to heel.

'Over here,' Mandy said worriedly.

James came and crouched beside her where she was stationed, keeping an eye on one of the ewes a short distance away.

'What is it?' he said.

Mandy frowned. 'That ewe,' she said. 'She's had twins but she only licked one of them. The other one is just lying there.'

James looked at her and Mandy felt her heart sink. 'No, James. It isn't dead. I'm sure it isn't.'

She looked across at the little bundle of wool lying on the short turf, neglected by its mother. It was a tiny black lamb, only minutes old. She had watched it being born.

'So what do we do?' said James.

Mandy shrugged. 'Dad said we mustn't frighten the ewe in a situation like this.'

James nodded. 'She would only bolt. We can't risk going near her, can we?'

Mandy considered. 'Maybe we can,' she said. 'After all, she's looking after the first lamb.'

'Maybe the other one just has to wait its turn,' said James.

Mandy shook her head. 'I've been watching,' she said. 'The poor little thing struggled all the way round to its mother's side but she just pushed it away. She's only interested in the first one.'

'So what can we do?' said James.

Mandy looked at him. 'You know what Dad said,' she said. 'If the lamb doesn't bond with the mother straight away then she won't feed it or look after it.'

James frowned. 'So we've got to try to get them together, one way or another,' he said. 'There isn't anything else for it.'

Mandy nodded. 'I think you're right,' she said. 'We have to risk it. But I wish Mr Spiller or Dad was here.'

James looked at his watch. 'Mr Spiller shouldn't be too long,' he said. 'Do you want to wait?'

But Mandy shook her head. The little black lamb was lying very still now. She didn't want to risk its life. 'I don't think we can afford to wait,' she said.

'OK,' said James.

'Quietly, James,' Mandy said. 'We don't want to scare the ewe.'

Softly, Mandy whistled for Jess. There was a swift flowing movement as the black and white dog came over the grass towards them, looking at Mandy with intelligent eyes.

'Hold her, Jess,' Mandy whispered to Jess.

Jess turned at once and went to the ewe, standing silently at her head, ready to stop her if she should bolt. But the ewe was too busy with the other lamb. She hardly took any notice of the sheepdog.

Quietly, Mandy and James approaching the ewe over the grass. Mandy kneeled beside the wet, little, black bundle on the ground. Gently she lifted the lamb closer to its mother. The lamb stirred in her arms as she did so and Mandy's heart fluttered. It was so small, so delicate.

The ewe took no notice. Mandy tried everything. She almost pushed the poor little lamb under the ewe's nose but it was no good. The ewe had time for only one lamb and it wasn't this little one.

It was when the ewe raised her head and gave an unmistakably angry bleat that Mandy knew it was useless.

'She's rejected it,' said James.

Mandy looked down at the little lamb. 'Poor little thing,' she said. 'What shall we do?'

James was brisk. 'First we get it cleaned up,' he said. 'Then we try and feed it.'

Mandy smiled. 'Of course,' she said. But she looked down again at the poor little thing. 'Poor lamb,' she said. 'We'll take care of you.'

James rummaged in the lambing bag for a rough towel. He handed it to Mandy and she wrapped it round the lamb, drying it, warming it. Although the day was mild, there was still a stiff breeze and this little thing was only just born.

As they carried the lamb to the shelter of the dry-stone wall Mandy looked back. The ewe was looking as proud as could be, suckling her other lamb. Mandy shook her head. Sometimes she just didn't understand nature.

But one thing was sure. They had to get some food into this lamb – and quickly. Carefully she put the lamb inside the lambing bag. It would be cosy there, lying on the fleecy lining. They started off down towards the farm.

Mandy had been in many a sheep farmer's kitchen at lambing time. It wasn't unusual to see three or four lambs tucked up in cardboard boxes and set close to the stove or the fire for warmth. The Spillers' kitchen was no different. There were three other little lambs being hand reared, Mandy and James were helping with that.

She settled the little lamb on its towel in front of the fire, then took the feeding bottle out of the lambing bag.

'I'll get some milk,' James said.

'Not straight from the fridge,' Mandy said. 'We should warm it a little.'

James nodded. 'I'll do that,' he said. 'You stay with the lamb.'

Mandy looked at the little creature lying in front of the fire. Even for a newborn lamb it was tiny. It was hard to believe that such a little thing could survive.

At last James came back with a saucepan of warm milk. Carefully, Mandy poured it into the feeding bottle and fixed the teat on. Then she sat down on the floor beside the lamb and lifted its little head.

'Here you are,' she said gently. 'It's milk. You'll like it.'

The lamb's eyes flickered. Then its nose twitched. Mandy rubbed the bottle against his lips and the lamb's tongue came out. Then his mouth fastened on the teat and he started to suck hungrily.

Mandy raised her face to James. 'Look,' she said. 'He's feeding.'

James grinned. 'Looks as if he's going to be all right,' he said.

Mandy looked at the stumpy little tail beginning to wag. 'He'll need lots of care though,' she said. 'He's so small. Smaller than any of the others.'

Mandy had just finished feeding the lamb when they heard the sound of an engine.

'That must be the Spillers,' said Mandy.

She laid the lamb gently down on the towel and followed James out into the farmyard.

Jenny was out of the van and across the yard like a whirlwind. 'We've got a baby!' she cried excitedly.

Mandy looked beyond her to Mrs Spiller. She was just getting out of the car with a white woolly bundle in her arms.

'It looks like another lamb,' James said and Mandy gave him a nudge.

'Oh, he's beautiful,' she said as Maggie Spiller proudly came to show the baby off.

Jack Spiller grinned. 'We're going to have our hands full now,' he said.

Jenny had run into the house to find Blackie and tell him the news.

Mandy looked at the proud father and mother. 'Oh,' she said, 'you have two new lambs as well.'

Jack Spiller's face beamed. 'That's good news,' he said. 'Just as long as they're healthy.' He turned to his wife. 'I'll just go and get those lambs from the kitchen. They're fit to go out in the field now. And you won't have time for that sort of thing, not now that you've got the baby to look after.'

Jenny ran out of the house. 'Daddy, Daddy,' she called. 'We've got a lamb.'

Jack Spiller grinned. 'We've got boxes full in there,' he said. 'But I'm just going to put them out. We won't have time to look after them.'

Jenny's face looked stricken. 'But it's so little, Daddy,' she said.

Jack grinned. 'They've been there a week and more,' he said. 'And we have to get rid of them. Your mum has the baby to look after now.'

Mandy looked at Jack Spiller. He didn't understand. Of course he didn't know about the new little lamb.

Jenny looked up at her father. 'Get rid of them? Even the little one?' she said. Her face was stricken.

Mandy turned quickly to Jack Spiller, but he was

taking his wife's things from the van, helping her into the house.

'All of them,' he said.

He'll understand, Mandy thought. *When he sees the lamb he'll understand.*

She looked round to explain to Jenny that her dad had made a mistake. But Jenny had gone.

Six

'We'll find someone to take care of it,' Mandy said. 'Won't we, James?'

They were standing in the Spillers' kitchen looking at the new lamb. James looked at Mandy's face. For a moment Mandy thought he was going to raise some difficulty. Then he nodded. 'Of course we will,' he said. 'Just give us a day or two.'

Jack Spiller shook his head. 'I can't ask Maggie to look after lambs just now – not with a new baby in the house. She's been doing enough of that recently. She's going to have her hands full as it is with me out all hours amongst the sheep.'

Mandy bit her lip. 'Today then,' she said. 'If

we haven't found anyone by this evening . . .' She stopped.

Jack Spiller nodded. 'OK,' he said. 'I'll give you till tonight. But I don't see how you're going to get anybody to take in a sickly little thing like that. Lambing is bad enough without having to look after anybody else's lambs.'

Mandy's mouth set in a determined line. She *would* find somebody to look after the lamb. After all, she had been an orphan and Adam and Emily Hope had looked after her. Her parents had been killed in a car crash when she was a baby and the Hopes had taken her in. She was adopted. Not that it felt like that. To her, Adam and Emily Hope were the best parents anyone could have.

'Till tonight,' she said to Jack Spiller. 'Don't forget – you promised.'

Mandy and James got their bikes from the old, tumbledown shed in the corner of the farmyard where they had left them. Mandy looked round. There was an old stone water trough in the far corner which looked solid enough. But the rest of the place was falling to bits.

'This place looks ready to fall down,' she said.

Mr Spiller came out of the house and called out to them. 'Don't leave your bikes in there. It's dangerous. I don't let anybody go in there.'

'Sorry, Mr Spiller,' Mandy said. 'We didn't know.'

Jack Spiller ran a hand through his hair. 'I forgot to mention it,' he said. 'I've had so much on my mind.' He looked at the old, tumbledown shed. 'First thing I do after the lambing is over is knock that old shed down.'

Mandy smiled. 'It won't be long now,' she said.

Jack Spiller grinned back. 'Nobody ever tells you what things are really like,' he said. 'Lambing looks easy enough but it's far from it.'

Mandy laughed. 'Animals are always a lot of work, Mr Spiller,' she said. 'But they're worth it.'

Jack Spiller smiled. 'You'll make a great vet some day, Mandy, if you've a mind to it.'

Mandy flushed with pleasure. 'I hope so,' she said. 'But right now it's finding a home for that little lamb that's worrying me.'

A shadow passed over Mr Spiller's face. 'It isn't that I'm being cruel,' he said. 'But that little lamb is a weakling. It would need a lot of attention – feeding every two hours or less – and even then it might not survive. Maggie just hasn't got the time or the energy for it just now – no more have I.'

Mandy nodded. 'I understand, Mr Spiller,' she

said. 'But we'll find somebody who has got the time and the energy. All we need is a few hours.'

Jack Spiller shook his head. 'You sound really confident,' he said.

James laughed. 'We haven't failed yet,' he said.

They waved as they pedalled down the track to the main road.

'Who on earth are we going to ask to take in a weakling lamb?' said James.

Mandy shrugged. 'I don't know,' she said. She looked hopeful. 'You don't think Mum and Dad—'

'No, I don't,' James interrupted her. 'You know your parents' rules about that.'

Mandy sighed. Her parents were quite strict about her bringing orphaned animals home. She knew they were right. Unless you said no to all of them you ended up taking all of them in. And then there would be no room for the animals that people brought to Animal Ark.

'It's a vet's practice,' Mrs Hope would say to Mandy, 'not a zoo.'

'What about Walter Pickard?' Mandy said.

James shook his head. 'Tom will be going home soon and he wouldn't be safe around a little lamb like that.'

Mandy sighed. 'I suppose that rules out a whole lot of people,' she said. 'Most people have a dog or a cat.'

'And Mr Spiller is right about the farmers,' said James. 'They're all too busy themselves at the moment to take on a sickly lamb.'

'It isn't really sickly,' said Mandy. 'Just extra small.'

James nodded. 'So it needs extra feeding – every two hours, was it?' he said. 'It wouldn't be so bad if it were sick – then we might be able to take it to Animal Ark.'

'Or the cottage hospital,' said Mandy, laughing. 'Matron could look after it along with the new babies. I've heard Matron never gets tired.'

Then she stopped talking.

James looked across at her. 'What is it?' he said. 'Have you thought of something.'

Mandy turned a shining face to him. 'I've had a brilliant idea,' she said. 'I don't know why I didn't think of it before. We'll take him to Gran! Gran and Grandad can look after him for a week or so – just until he's strong enough to be set on to another ewe.'

James's face lit up. 'Of course!' he said. 'That

would be perfect. Your Gran will love him.'

'I hope so,' Mandy said. 'I've a feeling it's our only chance.'

They found Grandad in the back garden, hoeing his vegetables.

'Hi, Grandad,' Mandy said as they parked the bikes in the back lane.

'Mandy!' said Grandad, his eyes lighting up with pleasure. 'And James. Just give me a minute and I'll put the kettle on.'

'No, no,' Mandy said quickly. 'Let me.'

Grandad's eyes twinkled. 'Uh-oh,' he said. 'Do I see somebody who wants a favour?'

Mandy laughed. 'Am I really that bad?' she said.

Grandad stuck his hoe in the ground beside him. 'You're not bad at all,' he said. 'It's just that your face gives you away. What is it you want?'

Mandy bit her lip. 'I would have to ask both of you,' she said. 'You and Gran.'

Grandad shook his head. 'Your Gran is off organising half the village over this hospital closure,' he said. 'She's called a meeting of the WI in the church hall.' Gran was chairperson of the Welford Women's Institute.

Mandy bit her lip.

'Can it wait?' Grandad said.

Mandy looked at James.

'Well,' said James, 'the sooner we find somebody to take it in the better.' Then he stopped.

Grandad laughed. 'I guess the secret is out now,' he said. 'Let me try and guess. You're looking for a home for some poor old animal you've found.'

'Not old, Grandad,' Mandy said. 'Actually it's young – very young.'

Grandad looked seriously at her. 'You know we can't take on an animal full time,' he said. 'Not the way we are with the camper van.'

Gran and Grandad had bought a camper van when Grandad retired. They were forever taking off on holiday in it. Gran said it made her feel like an explorer.

Mandy shook her head. 'It would only be for a week or so,' she said. 'Then it would be able to fend for itself – or not exactly fend for itself.'

'But it could go out in the top field,' said James.

'If we could set it on to another ewe,' Mandy finished.

Grandad looked from one to the other. Then his face cleared.

'You've been up at Fordbeck Farm helping Jack Spiller out,' he said.

Mandy nodded. 'It's a lamb, Grandad,' she said. 'A poor little lamb that has been rejected by its mother. It needs hand rearing for a week or so – just to get it started.'

'And we thought you and Mrs Hope would take it in,' said James.

'A lamb?' said Grandad.

Mandy looked at him. 'Of course,' she said. 'What did you think it was?'

Grandad chuckled. 'I was beginning to wonder,' he said. He pushed his cap to the back of his head and looked at them. 'Always up to something, you two,' he said. 'And there's always an animal there somewhere.'

'Will you do it, Grandad?' Mandy said eagerly. 'Do you think Gran will agree? It'll be an awful lot of work.'

Grandad's eyes twinkled. 'Tell you what,' he said. 'Let's go inside and get the kettle on and cut a bit of that freshly-baked fruit cake. We can have it ready for her when she comes back. Then, when she's had a nice cup of tea, we'll ask her.'

Mandy looked at her Grandad in mock outrage. 'And you say *I'm* bad?' she said.

Grandad laughed and tucked her arm into his as they walked down the path to the house. 'Can't think where you get it from,' he said, winking at James.

Seven

Mandy and James hurtled down the track to Fordbeck Farm, feet pedalling madly, bicycle wheels whizzing.

'It's all right!' Mandy called as they swept into the yard in front of the farmhouse.

James came to a skidding halt beside her and looked up at Jack Spiller. 'Mandy's Gran and Grandad are going to take the lamb,' he said. 'We've found a home for it. I told you we would.'

Jack Spiller didn't smile.

'What's wrong?' Mandy said.

Suddenly her heart felt heavy as lead. Surely the little animal hadn't died. It had been weak, yes, but not so weak as to die in a couple of hours. And Jack Spiller had promised to look after it until they came back.

Mandy stood there watching him as he shook his head.

'I don't understand it,' he said. 'It was there in front of the fire.'

'What do you mean, *was*?' said James, puzzled.

Jack Spiller spread his hands. 'Come and see,' he said.

Mandy and James followed him into the kitchen. Mrs Spiller was sitting in front of the fire, the baby cradled in her arms.

At her feet was a box with a clean piece of wadded sacking in it.

'There,' said Jack Spiller. 'That's where I left it. And when I came back half an hour later it had gone.'

Mrs Spiller shook her head. 'Poor little thing,' she said. 'It didn't look to me as if it could get very far on its own. Still, it's amazing how tough these hill sheep can be. Maybe the little thing wandered off.'

Mr Spiller looked completely puzzled. 'I don't see what else could have happened,' he said. 'But I would have sworn that little fellow wasn't strong enough.'

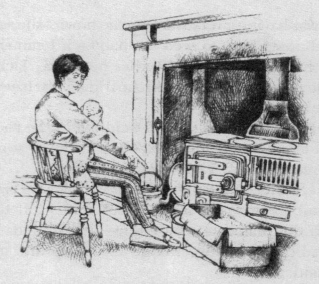

Mandy was worried. 'But if he's gone off, what will happen to him? Who will feed him?'

Mr Spiller shook his head. 'Even if he manages to find his way back to the other sheep, none of them will feed him,' he said.

'But haven't you looked for him?' said James.

Jack Spiller turned to him and Mandy saw how tired he looked.

'There have been a couple of ewes in a bad way up in the top field,' he said. 'I've been up there this last hour. But I didn't see the little fellow.'

Mandy turned to Mrs Spiller. But she shook her head.

'I was having a very welcome lie down,' she said. 'And now I have to feed the baby – if I can find that bottle.' She turned to her husband. 'Jack, I made up a feed and put it in the fridge. You haven't seen it, have you?'

Mrs Spiller stood up and went out of the room with the baby. 'I must have left it down somewhere,' she said. 'I'll lose my head next.'

Mr Spiller pursed his mouth. 'Look, you two,' he said. 'I'm really sorry about this. I left that lamb there and now he's gone.' He smiled. 'At least he was strong enough to get up and go,' he said.

Mandy felt troubled. 'Maybe he was,' she said. 'But he can't feed himself, not yet. And none of those other ewes will feed him.' She felt tears prick at the back of her eyes and blinked them back as she looked out of the window.

It was evening. The sky was darkening. And out on the hill was the little lamb she and James had saved, had found a home for.

'It won't last the night,' James said, putting all her fears into words. 'Not if it's out there on the hill with no mother to shelter it or feed it.'

All of a sudden Mandy made up her mind. 'Come on, James,' she said. 'We'll look for it.' She turned to Jack Spiller. 'Is that all right with you, Mr Spiller?'

Jack Spiller looked out of the window to where the light was waning. 'It'll be dark soon,' he said. Then he saw Mandy's face. 'But of course you can try. Take a torch.'

Gratefully, Mandy and James went with him while he looked for a powerful torch. Then they were running uphill towards the top field, searching the ditches on the way, looking behind dry-stone walls, into hedges. And all the time it was getting darker.

Neither of them said how hard it would be to find a tiny black lamb in the dark. Neither of them wanted to think about that. The wind blew chill and Mandy turned her collar up. *Poor little thing,* she thought. They had to find it.

'It's no good,' James said at last. 'We're only scaring the sheep. And that can't be good for the ones that are still to lamb.'

Mandy started to argue, then thought better of it. James was right. For nearly an hour they had searched the field, burrowed in ditches, torn their clothes and hands on thorn bushes. And now it was almost dark. But she didn't want to give up.

'Just one more look around, James,' she said.

But it was no good. Wearily they trudged down-hill – empty handed.

Jack Spiller met them at the farmyard. He didn't have to ask. He could see by the look on their faces that they hadn't found the lamb.

'He might not have survived anyway,' the farmer said, and Mandy nearly burst into tears.

Oh, yes, he would, she thought. *If he'd had a nice cosy place by the fire at Lilac Cottage and Gran and Grandad to fuss over him and look after him – he would have survived.*

But it was no good trying to say that to Mr Spiller. He was only trying to comfort them in his own way. And farmers had to be tough to survive. They couldn't become sentimental about losing lambs. It happened too often.

'Come in and have some milk and a biscuit before you go,' Jack Spiller said. 'And tell Maggie and Jenny I'll be in directly. I have to go and have a quick look at that old bulldozer in the far field before it gets too dark.'

Mandy and James walked into the warm and welcoming front kitchen. Maggie Spiller looked up at them and smiled. The baby was lying asleep in her arms.

'Isn't he lovely?' said Mandy.

Mrs Spiller smiled proudly and touched the baby's cheek gently with her fingertip. 'He is now,' she said. 'But he'll probably grow up just as wild as Jenny!' She looked up, still smiling. 'Where is Jenny?' she said.

Mandy looked round. 'Isn't she here?' she said.

Maggie Spiller's eyes looked at her sharply. 'I thought she had gone with you,' she said.

Mandy and James shook their heads. 'We haven't seen her,' Mandy said.

'But she was here in the kitchen just before you arrived,' Mrs Spiller said. She was looking distraught. Then her face cleared. 'Of course, she must be with her dad.'

She looked at Mandy and James and the smile died on her lips.

Mandy bit her lip. 'We met him outside, Mrs Spiller,' Mandy said. 'He said he was going over to have a look at the old bulldozer. He said we were to tell you and Jenny he wouldn't be long.'

Maggie Spiller's face was paper white. 'Me and Jenny?' she said. 'But Jenny isn't here. Jenny hasn't been in the house for the last hour or so.' Mandy and James looked at her as she sat, her face pale and drawn, holding the new baby closely to her.

'Where is Jenny?' Mrs Spiller said for the second time.

It was at that moment that they heard a crash. It came from outside in the yard. Mrs Spiller turned towards the sound.

'What was that?' she said.

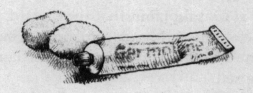

Eight

The sound seemed to echo around them. Mandy stood, rooted to the spot, her eyes still fixed on Mrs Spiller and the baby.

'What was that?' Mrs Spiller said again.

Her hand went to her mouth. Then she stood up quickly and tucked the sleeping baby into his carrycot. Her face was grim as she turned to them.

Mandy rushed to the window and looked out. Blackie went with her. He jumped up, resting his front paws on the window ledge. Then he was down again and running out into the yard.

'Blackie!' James called after him. But the Labrador took no notice.

There was dust still settling in the far corner of the farmyard.

'What is it?' said James.

'It's the old shed,' Mandy said, turning back into the room. 'The one Mr Spiller said was dangerous. It's collapsed.'

'That shed,' Mrs Spiller said. 'I've been telling Jack. Something needs to be done about it.' Her breath caught in her throat. 'You don't think . . . not Jenny . . . she can't be . . .' Then she was running for the door and out into the yard.

'Come on,' Mandy said to James. 'It might still be dangerous!'

They raced out into the yard and stood looking at the far corner where a heap of rubble lay. One side of the shed had collapsed entirely while the other side looked ready to collapse at any moment. Blackie prowled round the edges of the rubble.

'You don't think Jenny is in there, do you?' James said.

'Why should she be?' Mandy said. 'She was told to keep away from it. Mr Spiller said nobody was allowed to go near it.'

James nodded. 'You're right,' he said. 'But what about Mrs Spiller?'

Mrs Spiller was standing by the ruins of the

shed. She was calling Jenny's name.

Mandy went to stand beside her.

'It's all right, Mrs Spiller,' Mandy started to say.

'But where is Jenny?' Mrs Spiller said. She turned, distraught, looking for her daughter. She was more anxious than ever now.

'Look,' said Mandy. 'There's Mr Spiller coming.' She pointed towards the far field.

At once Mrs Spiller began to run towards her husband.

Mandy bit her lip. 'The poor Spillers,' she said. 'They aren't having much luck.'

James wasn't listening.

'James?' Mandy said. 'What is it?'

James shook his head. 'Nothing,' he said. 'I thought I heard something.'

Mandy looked at the ruins of the shed where Blackie was sniffing around. 'Blackie,' she called. 'Here, boy.'

The black Labrador took no notice.

'Call him, James,' Mandy said. 'The rest of that roof looks as if it's going to go any minute.'

James was watching Blackie intently.

'Look, Mandy,' he said. 'Look at the way Blackie's behaving. Sniffing, searching.'

Just then Blackie gave a short, sharp bark and

looked towards them. Then he began sniffing at a torn off sheet of corrugated iron.

'Come out of there, Blackie!' James said.

But the dog stayed firm where he was and barked again.

'What do you think he's found?' Mandy said.

James licked his lips and looked towards the far field. Jack Spiller had started running now. He was shouting something but he was still too far away for them to hear what it was. One thing was certain: Jenny wasn't with him.

'Do you think it's Jenny?' Mandy said.

'It might be,' James said. He looked at the sagging remains of the roof. The whole structure groaned and there was a sharp crack somewhere amongst the timbers.

'It's going to go any minute,' said Mandy. 'The whole thing is going to collapse!'

Blackie looked at them urgently, pawing the corrugated iron and barking.

Mandy and James looked at the remains of the overhanging roof, then at each other. The roof swayed.

'Come on,' said Mandy, 'We take an end each and heave. We'll be out of there in no time.'

Without giving themselves too much time to

think they scrambled over the collapsed wall into the shed. The roof creaked and groaned.

'Heave,' said Mandy as she grasped an end of the corrugated iron sheet.

James heaved. Blackie whimpered and began scrabbling at the edges of the sheet. Nothing happened.

'It's stuck,' said James, his face grim with effort.

Mandy nodded. 'It's wedged under that,' she said, pointing to a big stone that had fallen out of the wall. 'You shift the stone. I'll lift a corner of the sheet. We don't even know if Jenny is here.'

But, Mandy thought, *where else could she be?* The noise of the shed collapsing would have brought her running to see what had happened. The roof creaked again as James heaved on the stone and rolled it out of the way. Mandy bent and eased the corrugated iron sheet up a little. Then she gasped. A bright red gumboot lay at an awkward angle under the edge of the sheet.

Her face white, Mandy turned to James.

'I saw,' he said.

Then he was bending, straining to lift. Above them the roof swayed dangerously. Blackie whined and barked in warning.

'Again,' Mandy said through gritted teeth.

Slowly the corrugated iron sheet lifted. Mandy felt a sharp edge scrape along her forearm. With an almighty effort they pushed it to one side and looked down.

'Is she . . .' James didn't finish the sentence.

Mandy looked at Jenny. The little girl lay at an odd angle, her head twisted to one side. Blood flowed freely from a gash in her forehead and another in her leg. She looked very pale.

'Maybe we shouldn't move her,' Mandy said.

James looked up. Above them the roof beams cracked. A great cloud of dust fell and a stone dislodged itself from the wall, hit Mandy's knee and rolled, banging, on the corrugated iron. The roof creaked and groaned.

'It's going!' James said urgently. 'We've got to move her. We can't leave her.'

Grimly, Mandy nodded and together they bent and lifted the little girl's body. She was very light.

As they carried her through the door of the shed into the yard Jack Spiller came racing up, his face a mask of horror.

Grasping hold of Jenny, he took her from them, then urged Mandy and James in front of him across the yard.

Behind them the crash resounded, louder,

longer than before as the remains of the roof fell inwards.

Mandy and James stood there covered in dust, looking at the shed. Only one corner was intact now. The rest was hanging precariously in ruins.

'Is she hurt?' Mrs Spiller came running up, face white with strain.

Mr Spiller shook his head. 'She's bleeding badly,' he said. 'And she's unconscious. We have to get her to hospital as quickly as possible.'

At once everything was happening. Mandy rushed inside for fresh towels to wrap round Jenny's head and leg. Mrs Spiller collected the baby in his carrycot. Gently, Mr Spiller laid Jenny in the back of the van, wrapped in a rug, then jumped in and started to rev the engine.

Mrs Spiller leapt into the van beside Jenny, the baby on the floor beside her. She looked at Mandy and James. 'If you hadn't got her out . . .' she began.

'Go!' said Mandy as Mr Spiller revved the engine and put the car in gear. 'We'll follow on our bikes.'

The van leapt into life and surged off down the driveway.

Mandy and James looked at each other. They were filthy, and Mandy saw a long scratch on

James's cheek. She looked at herself. There was a graze on her arm.

'Come on,' said James. 'Let's go to the hospital. It's better than waiting here for news.'

The cottage hospital was warm and welcoming, its lights shining out through the gathering darkness. Mandy and James parked their bikes and ran up the steps into the hall.

A young nurse smiled at them, 'You two have been in the wars,' she said. 'Have you come to get yourselves patched up?'

Mandy frowned. 'No,' she said. 'It's Jenny, Jenny Spiller. Her mum and dad just brought her in.'

The smile disappeared from the nurse's face and Mandy felt her heart grow chilled.

'She's all right, isn't she?' said James.

The nurse pursed her lips. 'The doctor is with her now,' she said. 'And Matron.'

'Matron?' Mandy said. If Matron was there it must be serious.

'What's happening?' said James.

The nurse looked as if she wasn't going to tell them, then a voice said from the other end of the corridor, 'It's all right, Nurse Williams. I'll deal with this.'

Mandy and James looked up as the tall, straight figure of Matron came quietly down the corridor. Mandy gulped; Johnny Pearson was right. Matron was looking at them with a severe expression. She had neat, grey hair and piercing blue eyes. She was looking very serious indeed.

'Mr and Mrs Spiller told me how you rescued Jenny,' she said as she reached them.

'Is she going to be all right?' said Mandy.

Matron pursed her lips. 'We'll know very soon,' she said. 'Jenny has concussion and she's lost a lot of blood. She also has a broken leg. She's having a transfusion at the moment.'

'A blood transfusion?' Mandy said and gulped.

Matron's expression softened a little.

'Her parents are in my office with the baby,' she said. 'I don't think they should be disturbed just at the moment. Why don't you go into the waiting-room if you want to wait and see how she is?'

Mandy and James nodded. 'Yes, we'd like to wait,' said Mandy.

Matron nodded understandingly. 'Of course you would,' she said.

The waiting-room was tiny. It was brightly-painted and there was a pile of magazines and a box of children's toys in the corner. Mandy didn't feel like reading.

She and James sat there in silence. There didn't seem anything to say. It was just a matter of waiting.

Nurse Williams looked in on them after half an hour.

'There you are,' she said. 'Now I hope you two aren't worrying too much.'

Mandy looked at her hopefully. 'Any news?' she asked.

Nurse Williams pursed her lips. 'No news is good news,' she said. 'But it's lucky her mum and dad got her here so quickly. If they'd been much later that little girl would have lost too much blood. As it is, they got that transfusion started just in time.'

Mandy's mouth went dry with fright. It had been much worse than they'd thought.

'Nurse Williams,' said a voice from the door, 'I wonder if you would look in on the children's ward. Mary Anne Malloy wants to show you her new nightie.' It was Matron, looking disapproving.

Nurse Williams flushed to the roots of her hair. 'Another new nightie?' she said. 'She must have dozens of them.' And she bustled off.

'Little Jenny is going to be fine,' Matron said firmly. 'You are not to worry about her.' She looked at Mandy. 'I've telephoned your grandmother, Mandy. She is going to let your parents and James's know where you are.'

'Oh, thank you, Matron,' Mandy said. 'I didn't think.'

Matron smiled. 'I know you're worried,' she said, 'but that doesn't mean we should worry your parents too.'

'No, Matron,' Mandy said meekly. She felt quite sorry for young Nurse Williams.

Then she looked at Matron. Matron's face softened. She turned in the doorway as she was leaving. 'I'll put some antiseptic on those cuts before you go,' she said.

'Oh,' said Mandy. 'It's nothing. They don't hurt.'

Matron merely smiled. Then she was gone.

'They always say that, don't they?' James said gloomily when Matron had gone.

'What?' asked Mandy.

'That people will be fine,' James said.

Mandy nodded. 'But she will be. I know she will.'

At last there was the sound of voices in the corridor and the whimper of a very young baby crying.

'The Spillers!' Mandy and James said together and shot out of the waiting-room.

Mandy looked at Maggie Spiller. She was crying. Mandy's heart lurched. Then she realised she was smiling as well.

Mrs Spiller saw Mandy and came over and put her arms round her.

'She's going to be all right, thanks to you two,' Mrs Spiller said. 'She needed some blood really quickly but she'll be OK now.'

Mandy smiled up at her, then she looked at Mr Spiller. But he wasn't smiling. His face was grim.

He came and stood in front of them. 'I can't thank you two enough,' he said. 'But right now I'm going home to get that bulldozer fixed, and as soon as it's fixed I'm going to knock down the rest of that shed.'

Mrs Spiller looked at the baby. 'This little one needs feeding,' she said. 'Jenny is asleep and she isn't to be disturbed tonight. Come on, you two. Put your bikes in the back of the van and we'll take you home.'

Mandy and James looked at her gratefully. Suddenly they were both quite tired.

'One moment,' said Matron. She eyed them up and down. 'I wanted to put some antiseptic on those cuts.'

'Oh, don't bother,' James said at once. 'They don't hurt at all.'

'Anyway Mum will do it,' Mandy said, rolling down her sleeve to hide the graze on her arm.

'Mandy's mum is a vet,' James said.

Matron smiled thinly. 'I should hope you appreciate the difference between people and mere animals,' she said.

Mere animals! Mandy thought, outraged. She opened her mouth to protest but the Spillers were leaving.

'What does she mean "mere animals"?' she said indignantly to James as he bundled her out of the door towards the van.

'Shh!' said James. 'She'll hear you.'

'I don't care if she does,' said Mandy. 'Mere animals, indeed. Huh! It was Blackie who knew Jenny was under all that rubble. If it hadn't been for Blackie, we wouldn't have been able to rescue Jenny. Mere animals! *Wonderful* animals is more like it!'

Nine

'So that's why I was so late home,' Mandy finished. 'And that's why you won't have that little lamb to look after.' She looked round the faces at the table.

Gran and Grandad had come for supper at the Hopes' cottage.

'We'd have been happy to look after the little fellow,' said Grandad, 'but I must say we were more worried about you.'

'Matron didn't go into details when she phoned,' Gran said.

'With all that going on, I don't think being late home is very important,' Emily Hope said smiling.

Mandy noticed she didn't say anything about

the lost lamb. There was no point. A lamb as small as that could never survive on its own.

'Poor Mrs Spiller,' Gran said. 'What a worry for her!'

'Farms can be dangerous places for children,' Grandad said. 'Especially children not brought up on a farm.'

'Mr Spiller had told Jenny never to go into that shed,' Mandy said.

Mr Hope shook his head. 'I'm sure he did,' he said. 'But I must say I can't blame him for wanting to bulldoze it as soon as possible.' He looked at Mandy. 'And as for you and James rushing in there . . .'

Mandy looked guilty. She wished James was still here but he had gone home. 'There was nothing else to do,' she said.

Her dad smiled but she could see the worry behind his eyes. 'Of course not,' he said. 'And it all turned out for the best. I just wish you wouldn't get yourselves into these scrapes.'

Mandy bit her lip but didn't say anything. She had tried to make as little as possible of the danger but Jack Spiller had praised her and James to the skies when he had brought her and James back to Animal Ark.

'Time enough for all that tomorrow,' Mrs Hope said. 'Mandy, your eyes are almost closing, you're so tired.'

Mandy yawned. 'What about the animals?' she said.

'The medications are all done,' Mrs Hope said. 'Don't worry about that.' She looked at her daughter. 'I think you should have a bath to ease those bruises and I'll come up later and put some cream on your cuts.'

Mandy pulled a face. 'Matron wanted to put antiseptic on them,' she said.

Mum laughed. 'I'll bet she did,' she said. 'Don't worry, this cream won't sting.'

Mandy yawned again as she got up from the table.

'Good night, Gran,' she said but Gran didn't answer. She was staring into space.

'Gran?' Mandy said.

'Oh, yes, sorry,' Gran said. 'I was miles away.'

Grandad laughed. 'Maybe you need an early night as well,' he said.

But Gran was as bright as a button. 'No,' she said. 'It's just that something occurred to me.' She turned to Mandy. 'You said that Matron told you Jenny got her blood transfusion just in time?' she said.

Mandy shook her head. 'It wasn't Matron, it was the nurse who said that.'

Gran nodded. 'That sounds more like it,' she said. 'Matron would be far too discreet to say a thing like that.'

'What are you getting at?' said Grandad.

Gran turned to him. 'I was wondering what would have happened if Jenny hadn't been able to have that blood transfusion when she did.'

Mandy shivered. 'But she did, Gran. That's all that matters,' she said.

Grandad laid a hand on Gran's arm. 'I know you feel really sorry for the Spillers and the trouble they've had lately, but the little girl is on the mend now.'

'Only because she got that blood transfusion,' said Gran.

Grandad looked puzzled. 'Of course,' he said.

'But don't you see?' said Gran. 'If Jenny hadn't got that transfusion so quickly she might have died. What I'm getting at is, if the accident had happened after they closed the cottage hospital, Jenny wouldn't have got that transfusion so quickly. What happens if there is another accident like this – after the hospital is closed?'

Mandy looked at her. 'Of course,' she said. 'I didn't think of that.'

Gran nodded. Her face was very serious. 'As your Grandad says, farms can be dangerous places and accidents can easily happen.' She looked round the table. 'We need that hospital,' she said. 'It really is a life-line for us. And I'm going to make sure that we keep it.'

Mandy threw her arms round Gran's neck and hugged her. 'And I'll help you,' she said. 'What do you want me to do?'

Gran squeezed Mandy's hands. 'Tomorrow I'll go and see Marion Timpson,' she said.

'Who?' said Mandy.

Gran's eyes twinkled. 'Matron,' she said. 'She isn't happy about this closure business. In fact she's hopping mad about it.'

Mandy blinked. She couldn't imagine the cool and frosty Matron hopping mad about anything.

'The campaign is all very well as it is,' Gran said, 'but we aren't making an impression on people. We've got to get the message across. That hospital is important. It isn't like other things. Keeping it open could make the difference between life and death. And if it takes a fight to keep it open then I'm ready to fight.

And so will a whole lot of other people in Welford and Walton.'

Gran paused, then her eyes lit up. 'In fact,' she went on, 'if they're trying to close one cottage hospital, you can bet your boots they're trying to close others. I wouldn't be surprised if there are a whole lot of communities facing this at the moment.' Her head came up. 'What we need,' she said, 'is a national campaign. We need to get the media on to this. Press coverage, TV. You wait and see. Once I'm finished we'll have a whole lot of support from all over the country, you see if we don't. Close our cottage hospital? Over my dead body!' Gran finished triumphantly.

Mandy gave Gran an extra hug. Adam Hope began to clap and Emily Hope and Grandad joined in.

'What a speech!' Mr Hope said. 'One thing's for sure, we're all behind you.'

'Just let us know,' Mrs Hope said. 'Fund-raising, posters, you name it – we'll help.'

Grandad didn't say anything. Mandy looked at him, puzzled. Then she saw the pride in his eyes as he looked at his feisty little wife. 'Come on, Dorothy,' he said to Gran. 'Time we were off.' He turned to Mrs Hope. 'I'll take this firebrand out of your kitchen, Emily, before she sets the whole place alight!'

Emily Hope laughed. 'You don't fool us,' she said. 'You're as proud as Punch of your firebrand. And she can set our kitchen alight any time she likes.'

'Ouch!' said Mandy as she emerged from sleep next morning. She looked round her, puzzled for a moment. Why did she feel stiff and sore? Then she remembered the events of the day before and sighed in relief. Jenny was all right. James and she were going to the hospital today to check up on her.

It was a moment before Mandy remembered the little black lamb. Her mouth turned down. There was no way the little fellow could have survived a night outside with no mother to protect him. Mandy would just have to put him out of her mind. There was nothing else for it.

Mandy threw back her duvet and swung her legs out of bed. She winced again as she did so. There was an ugly looking bruise on her knee.

'At least Matron won't see it,' she said to herself as she crossed the room towards the window.

Leaning across the pine table in the window,

Mandy drew the flowery curtains aside and looked down into the garden.

A whole family of rabbits scuttled around, tearing up mouthfuls of grass, chasing each other in and out of bushes. Mandy laughed at their antics and turned back to her room. With its old pine furniture and posters of animals it was her haven.

'Mandy,' a voice called from downstairs.

Mandy threw open her bedroom door and leaned over the banister to look down the twisty stair. 'Good morning,' she called back to her mother.

'James has just phoned,' her mum called back. 'He'll be over in half an hour.'

'Good,' said Mandy. 'We're going to the hospital to see Jenny.'

'You might see Gran,' Mrs Hope called back. 'She's going over to see Matron this morning. She's fizzing with energy over this campaign. Scrambled eggs for breakfast?'

Mandy laughed at the change of subject. 'Yummy!' she said. 'I'll be there in five minutes.'

A quick shower, a clean shirt and a fresh pair of jeans and Mandy was running downstairs, her hair still damp.

Mr Hope emerged from the door that led to

the surgery. 'You've done the morning medications,' Mandy said. 'Did I oversleep?'

Her dad grinned and ruffled her hair. 'Don't you think you deserved an extra half hour after yesterday?' he said.

Mandy frowned. 'I like helping you,' she said.

'I know you do,' said Mr Hope. 'And you can give your mum a hand with the evening medications. I'm going to be out until quite late doing tuberculin injections.'

'Hard work,' Mandy said. 'But worth it.' She knew the injections helped to stop cows from passing on tuberculosis. 'How is Tom?'

Mr Hope grinned. 'Back to his old anti-social ways. Honestly, they might talk about a cat having nine lives but that animal has twice that at least.'

'I'll just pop in and see him before breakfast,' Mandy said.

A bright red head peeked round the door, 'Oh, no you won't,' said Emily Hope. 'Breakfast is on the table. You can go and see Tom afterwards – and add a few scratches to the ones you've already got.' She looked worriedly at her daughter, then her face cleared. 'You look completely recovered,' she said.

Mandy grinned. 'Oh, I'm fine,' she said, 'But I'm starving.'

Mrs Hope laughed. 'That's a good sign at least,' she said. 'Come on, before the eggs get cold.'

Mandy followed her mum into the kitchen. The sun shone through the windows, making the copper pans sparkle where they hung on the oak beams. The table was laid with a fresh, red-checked cloth and on it stood a plate mounded with honey coloured toast, a dish of pancakes and a great heap of butter-yellow scrambled eggs in a blue bowl.

'Terrific!' Mandy said with feeling.

Mandy was just polishing off the last pancake when she heard the sound of a bike scattering the gravel in the drive.

'It's James,' said Mrs Hope, looking out of the window. 'And Blackie.'

'I'm off,' said Mr Hope. 'And don't you two get up to any mischief today. Your mum and I have had enough excitement for one week.

Mandy grinned. 'Don't worry,' she said. 'James and I have had enough as well.'

'Enough what?' said a voice and James appeared round the kitchen door, shoving his brown, floppy hair out of his eyes.

'Excitement,' said Mandy.

'Too right,' James said. 'I had to promise Mum I

would behave before she would let me out. Behave? We didn't do anything wrong.'

Mr Hope laughed as he gathered up his vet's bag and passed James on the way to the door. 'Parents always blame you when they're worried about you,' he said. 'You just have to put up with it.'

James grinned back. 'I suppose so,' he said. His eyes went to the table. 'Did you have pancakes?' he said.

Emily Hope looked at Mandy and James and shook her head. 'I don't know where you two put all the food you eat,' she said. 'There isn't an ounce of fat on either of you.'

'I'll just be going,' Mr Hope said, sidling out of the door.

Mandy laughed. Mrs Hope was always getting at him about his weight. It wasn't that he was fat – just not thin. And he did jog to try and keep his weight down.

'Bye, Dad,' she called after him.

Mrs Hope looked at her watch.

'Surgery in half an hour,' she said. 'Tell you what. You two go and look in on Tom and I'll make another batch of pancakes. I'll call you when they're ready.'

'Great,' said James. 'You make the best pancakes, Mrs Hope.'

Mrs Hope grinned. 'Flattery will get you everywhere, James,' she said. She looked at Blackie. 'I suppose you want some too?' she said.

Blackie wagged his tail and Mandy just managed to catch the butter dish before it was swept off the table.

Tom was, as Mr Hope had said, on the mend.

'Ow!' said James as he lifted the cat out of the cage.

'His claws are really sharp,' Mandy said.

James sucked his hand. 'Don't I know it,' he said. 'What a monster!'

Mandy looked at the old cat. 'He isn't a monster,' she said. 'Just a bit grumpy.'

'Grumpy is pretty normal for Tom,' James said.

Mandy frowned. 'I hope Jenny is back to normal today,' she said. 'Poor little girl. She must have got a terrible shock.'

James put Tom back in his cage. 'Let's go this morning,' he said. 'As soon as we've had the pancakes. Matron must let us see her today.'

Mandy nodded. Surely Jenny would be well enough to have visitors today.

Mrs Hope called them back just as they were leaving. 'Take this to Jenny,' she said, holding out a prettily-wrapped parcel.

'Thanks, Mum,' said Mandy. 'What is it?'

'Soaps,' said Mrs Hope, 'shaped like flowers. I thought she would like them.'

'She will,' said Mandy.

'Mum sent some fruit,' said James.

'And I've got a card and a little game here for her,' Jean Knox said. 'Just hold on while I write the card.'

Mandy looked at the receptionist with affection as Jean caught the glasses swinging from their chain round her neck, put them on, and wrote a message on the card.

'Thanks, Jean,' she said. 'It'll be like Christmas.'

James called to Blackie and they were off down the track from Animal Ark and heading for the Walton Road.

They passed Walter Pickard on his way to the church for the bell-ringing practice. He was carrying a big bunch of flowers from his garden. 'Your grandad tells me you've been in the wars, young miss,' he called to Mandy.

Mandy grinned and stopped her bike. 'So has Tom,' she said.

Walter scratched his head. 'You'd think he'd be old enough to know better, wouldn't you?' he said. 'Your mum says I can have him back tomorrow – if I can keep him out of trouble.'

Mandy laughed at the idea of keeping Tom out of trouble.

'We've been told to stay out of trouble as well,' James said gloomily.

Walter laughed. 'Where are you two young ones off to?'

'The cottage hospital,' Mandy said. 'To see Jenny Spiller.'

Walter grinned. 'At least you can't get into any trouble in a hospital,' he said. Then he shook his head. 'Bad business, that,' he said. 'But you two did well from what I hear. You tell the little lass I'm asking for her,' he went on. He looked at the flowers he was carrying. 'I was taking these along to the church for the WI ladies to arrange,' he said. 'But I reckon young Jenny would like them. Here you are, young miss,' And he handed the bunch of flowers to Mandy.

'Oh, Mr Pickard, thank you,' Mandy said as she put the flowers in her bicycle basket. 'They're lovely. Jenny will be so pleased.'

Julian Hardy, who owned the Fox and Goose,

stepped out of his pub as he saw them coming. 'How's little Jenny?' he said.

Mandy smiled. News certainly got round fast in Welford. 'We're just going to see her,' she said.

'Wait there, then,' said Mr Hardy and disappeared into the pub. He was out again in a moment carrying a bottle of orange squash. 'Give her this from me,' he said.

It was like that all through the village. Mrs McFarlane from the post office saw them passing and called them in while she made up a pile of comics to take to Jenny. By the time they got to the hospital their arms were full of presents. Mandy looked at Blackie trotting along beside them. She smiled. She had the feeling that Blackie might be the best present of all. Jenny was so fond of him.

'And Mr Spiller thought they might not be accepted in these parts,' Mandy said to James.

'What?' said James.

Mandy explained as they rode along. 'One of the reasons they kept themselves to themselves was that he thought they would be looked on as not really country folk. You know, with him losing his job in the town and all. He thought he might be resented.'

Mandy looked at the pile of gifts in her bicycle basket.

'Well,' she said. 'They can't very well think that people don't care about them now!'

Ten

'Where do you think you're going with that dog?'
said a voice.

Mandy and James turned.

It was Matron, looking really forbidding.

'What does she mean "that dog"?' James
whispered to Mandy. 'Blackie isn't "that dog".'

'Shh,' said Mandy. 'She'll hear you.'

'I certainly did hear you, James Hunter,'
said Matron as she strode down the corridor
towards them.

'We brought Blackie to see Jenny,' Mandy said.

'Yes,' said James. 'She and Blackie get on
really well.'

Matron stopped in front of them and folded her arms. 'No animals are allowed inside the hospital,' she said.

'But why not?' said Mandy.

Matron looked shocked. 'Why not?' she said. 'Because they're unhygienic, that's why not!' she said. 'They'd bring all kinds of nasty germs into the hospital. We've got sick people here, you know.'

Mandy frowned. 'We wouldn't let him jump on the beds or anything,' she said. 'And besides, sick people are supposed to get better quicker if they have pets.'

'That's right,' James said. 'I read that somewhere. Pets are good for sick people.'

Matron drew herself up. 'Not in this hospital,' she said. She looked at Mandy. 'I was having a long talk with your grandmother this morning about trying to save the hospital,' she said. 'Your grandmother said you were helping her.'

Mandy nodded. 'James is helping too,' she said. 'We've done lots of posters and leaflets and things.'

Matron sniffed. 'Fine way to help,' she said, 'bringing animals into the hospital. That's just the kind of thing that would do us a lot of harm. If we're going to run a campaign to save the hospital we have to be sure everything is run perfectly. We

can't have animals running around everywhere. Now put that dog outside – and wash your hands before you go into the ward.' And Matron stomped off down the corridor.

'Gosh,' said James. 'You'd think we'd brought in a whole zoo full of animals instead of one harmless dog.'

Blackie looked up at them with mournful eyes.

'Don't take any notice, Blackie,' Mandy said. 'We don't think you're full of germs.'

They took Blackie outside and left him tied to a tree in the garden before they went back into the hospital to find Jenny.

'Don't stay long,' said Nurse Williams.

Mandy and James looked at her.

'She *is* better, isn't she?' Mandy said.

The nurse smiled. 'She's still very tired,' she said. 'But her broken leg should mend well. It isn't like poor Johnny Pearson's. That was a really bad break.' She frowned. 'I think something is worrying her, though, but she won't say what it is.' Then she looked at the pile of presents Mandy and James were carrying. 'I should think that lot will cheer her up,' she said.

'Have Mr and Mrs Spiller been in today?' Mandy asked.

The nurse nodded. 'They were here first thing,' she said. 'Isn't that baby a darling? They left not long ago. Mr Spiller said he had to get back.' The nurse smiled. 'Funny man – he said he had a bit of bulldozing to do.'

Mandy frowned as they followed the nurse down the corridor. What could be worrying Jenny?

'You go ahead,' said Nurse Williams as she showed them into the bright, sunny ward. She took the bunch of flowers Mandy was carrying. 'Aren't these lovely?' she said. 'I'll just put them in water.' And she walked briskly back down the corridor.

The children's ward was quite small – only six beds, and three of them were occupied.

Poor Johnny had his leg in traction. His curly, red head turned as they came in and he gave them an impish grin. Mandy and James grinned back.

'How are you, Johnny?' Mandy said as they passed his bed.

'Bored,' said Johnny. 'There's nothing to do.'

'You could read,' said Mandy.

'I've read all my comics twice,' Johnny said. His eye fell on the bundle of things in Mandy's hands. 'Is that this week's comics?' he said.

Mandy nodded, grinning. 'Maybe Jenny will let

you read them when she's finished with them,' she said.

Johnny looked at Jenny over the sling his leg was caught up in. 'I bet she won't even read them,' he said. 'She just lies there and cries.'

Mandy opened her mouth to say something but a voice piped up from the next bed.

'There's somebody she wants to see but when you ask her who it is she won't tell you.'

Mandy looked at the next bed. A plump little fair-haired girl was perched on the end of it, brushing the hair of a fair-haired doll. Mandy didn't recognise her.

'Hi,' she said. 'I'm Mary Anne Malloy. I've had my appendix out. I've seen it. They showed it to me after the operation. It was disgusting!'

Mandy blinked and heard James laugh beside her.

'You didn't want to take it home in a jar or anything?' he said.

Mary Anne carried on brushing her doll's hair. The doll had a pink nightie on, just like Mary Anne's.

'No way,' she said. She looked up at them. 'I wish Jenny felt a bit better. I offered to let her play with Gilda,' she held up the doll, 'but she didn't want to.' Mary Anne sighed.

'That was kind of you,' said Mandy. 'But maybe she isn't well enough yet.'

Mary Anne smiled. 'That's probably it,' she said. 'I felt awful for the first couple of days after I had my appendix out. I was an emergency case.'

'What, with an ambulance and everything?' James said.

Mary Anne nodded proudly. 'Daddy says they stopped all the traffic on the Walton roundabout.' She gave them a huge smile. 'Fancy that,' she said.

Mandy couldn't help laughing. 'Fancy,' she said. 'Look, Mary Anne, we're going to see Jenny now.'

'Tell her she can play with Gilda any time she likes,' said Mary Anne.

'We shall,' said Mandy.

'She's a riot,' James said as they made their way across to Jenny's bed. It was set next to the french windows that opened up into the garden at the back of the cottage hospital. The sun came streaming through the light, flowered curtains on to the neat bed where Jenny lay. Her face was turned away from them.

'Maybe she's asleep,' said Mandy.

But at the sound of her voice the head on the pillow turned and Jenny gave them a weak smile.

'Hello,' said Mandy. 'We've brought you some presents. Everybody is asking about you.'

Jenny didn't say anything.

James looked uncomfortable. 'Is there anything you want?' he said. 'Anything we can do for you?'

Jenny shook her head and a big fat tear ran down her cheek. She moved her lips and said something but so low that they couldn't hear what it was.

'What?' said Mandy.

Jenny turned to her. 'Blackie,' she said.

Mandy bit her lip. 'We brought him,' she said. 'But Matron wouldn't let us bring him in. She won't allow animals into the hospital.'

Jenny's face had brightened but now with Mandy's last words she looked sad again.

'He's dead, isn't he?' she said.

Mandy was shocked. 'Dead?' she said. 'Of course he isn't dead. He's outside, tied to a tree.'

Jenny shook her head. 'You're just saying that,' she said and another big tear ran down her cheek.

Mandy and James looked at each other as Jenny turned her face away.

'Why on earth does she think he's dead?' said James.

Mandy shrugged. 'I don't know,' she said. 'But she's obviously worried about it. She won't get better if she goes on worrying like this.'

'But we can't bring Blackie in,' said James. 'You heard Matron. She'd kill us.'

Mandy nodded, trying to think. Her eyes rested on the french windows beside Jenny's bed.

'We don't have to bring him in,' she said. 'We just have to bring him round to the french windows. Then Jenny can see he isn't dead.'

'Brilliant,' said James. 'You wait here with Jenny. I'll go and fetch Blackie.'

Mandy nodded and James went quickly out of the ward.

'James has gone to get Blackie,' Mandy said to the little girl. 'You wait and see. He'll be here in a minute.'

Jenny's eyes looked bright with tears. 'Are you sure?' she said.

Mandy nodded. 'I promise,' she said.

There was a tap on the french windows. Mandy went over and unlatched them.

'Look, Jenny,' she said. 'Here's Blackie come to see you.'

Eagerly the little girl sat up in bed and leaned forward to see. Then her face crumpled. Her mouth drooped and she said, 'Not that Blackie. I want *my* Blackie.'

Mandy looked at her in astonishment.

'Your Blackie?' she said. 'What do you mean?'

Jenny shook her head, the tears running down her cheeks. 'My Blackie,' she repeated. 'My little black lamb.'

Light began to dawn on Mandy.

'What's going on?' said James from beyond the window. 'Is she pleased?'

Mandy shook her head. 'There's a problem,' she said. 'It seems we've got the wrong Blackie.'

'What?' said James. In his surprise he stepped over the sill into the ward. Blackie came with him.

'Oh!' said Mary Anne from her bed. 'What a lovely dog. Can I pet him?'

James nodded absently and Mary Anne trotted over to pet Blackie.

Mandy turned to Jenny. 'Your lamb,' she said. 'Is that the one that went missing, the one we left in the kitchen? The tiny one?'

Jenny nodded. 'Daddy said we couldn't have it. He said it was too much trouble – it would have to go.' She looked up, her little face fixed. 'I took him away,' she said. 'I hid him. Then I took one of the baby's bottles and some milk to feed him – just the way you said you did. Just the way Mum did with those other lambs. I know how. Mum showed me.'

James started to speak but Mandy shook her head. Very gently she sat down on Jenny's bed and put her arm round her.

'Jenny,' she said, 'where did you hide the lamb?'

Jenny's eyes filled with tears again. 'If I tell you then Daddy will get rid of him,' she said.

Mandy hesitated. There was no easy way of putting this. 'But, Jenny,' she said, 'if your Blackie is all alone then he'll get sick. Lambs as small as that need someone to take care of them.'

Again Jenny shook her head. 'Daddy would be angry,' she said.

Mandy sighed. 'But how can we find Blackie and bring him to see you if we don't know where he is?'

Jenny looked up at her. 'You wouldn't tell anybody?' she said. 'You would bring him here so that I could see he was all right?'

'Cross my heart,' said Mandy. 'And I'll look after him until you get out of hospital. I promise.'

Jenny looked at her again. 'I put him in the shed. The old one.'

It took a moment for Mandy to realise what the little girl was saying.

'The old shed?' she said. 'The one you got hurt in?'

Jenny looked puzzled and Mandy realised she didn't remember how she got hurt. She had been unconscious when they had found her.

'You mean the one your dad told you not to go into? The tumbledown shed. That one?'

Jenny nodded. 'He wouldn't let anybody go in there so I knew nobody would find Blackie.'

Mandy and James looked at each other. 'Where did you put him?' Mandy said.

Jenny frowned. 'Right at the back,' she said. 'In the water trough, so that he couldn't run away and get hurt.'

Mandy conjured up a mental picture of the shed as she had last seen it. The water trough was right over at the back. As far as she could remember the roof was still intact at that point.

It was then that James said, 'The bulldozing – remember what Nurse Williams said?'

Mandy turned to him.

'Oh, no,' she said.

'What is it?' said Jenny.

Quickly Mandy smiled. She couldn't very well tell the little girl that her father was going to bulldoze the shed that very afternoon.

'It's nothing,' Mandy said. 'But we have to go.' She looked at James.

'We have to go and get your Blackie,' James said to Jenny.

Jenny's face lit up. 'And bring him back.'

'If he's well enough,' Mandy said. 'You just get better now, won't you?'

Jenny smiled and snuggled down in bed. 'And don't let Daddy put him out, will you?' she said.

Mandy shook her head. 'He won't do that,' she said. She turned to James. 'We'd better phone – just in case.'

'I don't believe my eyes!' a voice said – a familiar voice.

Mandy and James turned. Matron stood at the door of the ward. 'How dare you disobey my orders?' she said.

'We didn't,' said James. Then he looked at where Mary Anne was playing with Blackie. 'Oh, dear,' he said.

'We have to make a phone call,' Mandy said.

Matron looked outraged. 'Phone call!' she said. 'I've never heard such cheek in my life. Phone call, indeed. You will put that animal outside, then you will report to me in my office.' And she turned on her heel and left the ward.

Matron was obviously not used to being disobeyed.

Mandy looked at James in horror.

'We have to get in touch with the Spillers,' James said.

'She won't let us. She won't listen,' said Mandy. 'You heard her. She's on the warpath.'

'So what do we do?' said James.

Mandy shrugged. 'There's only one thing to do,' she said. 'We make a run for it. We've got to get to Fordbeck Farm before Mr Spiller bulldozes that shed!'

Eleven

Mandy's legs were aching by the time the track to Fordbeck Farm came into view.

'What's that noise?' she said as they rounded the bend in the track, earth spurting beneath their wheels.

'Look!' shouted James as he hurtled down the track towards the farm. Mandy followed his gaze.

'Oh, no!' she gasped. 'Hurry!'

Jack Spiller was driving the bulldozer through the gate at the back of the farm into the farmyard. He was making straight for the shed.

'Too late!' James yelled over the increasing roar of the bulldozer.

Mandy thought of Jenny. 'We can't be too late,' she said.

Together they hurtled through the farm gates right in front of the bulldozer.

'Stop,' they yelled. 'Stop!'

Mandy saw Jack Spiller's face look down at them, astonished. He swerved the bulldozer to one side, put on the brakes and leapt down from the cab.

'What the devil do you two think you're doing?' he yelled. 'Have you any idea how dangerous that was?'

Mandy leapt off her bike and ran to him. 'Mr Spiller,' she said. 'You must listen. It's Jenny.'

At once Jack Spiller stopped shouting. His face went white. 'Jenny?' he said. 'Is she all right? What's happened?'

Mandy shook her head. 'Nothing,' she said. 'At least she's so unhappy because of the lamb – the one that disappeared – Jenny took it – she hid it in the shed. It's still there.'

'Say all that again slowly,' said Jack Spiller.

Mandy did, with James's help. Blackie arrived, panting, as they finished talking.

'So you see,' Mandy finished, 'she's so worried about that little lamb, she isn't getting better. We promised her that we'd bring the lamb to see her.

It's in that shed, Mr Spiller. We told Jenny we'd look after it – and we will, if it's still alive.'

Jack Spiller looked undecided. 'That place is dangerous,' he said.

Mandy nodded. 'I know,' she said. 'But the lamb is hidden in the old water trough.'

'At the back of the shed?' Mr Spiller said.

'Yes, the roof hasn't fallen in back there,' said James.

Mandy watched as Mr Spiller weighed up the chances of finding the lamb alive.

'It's just that she wanted that little lamb so much,' said Mandy.

Jack Spiller made up his mind. 'Wait here,' he said. 'And don't move.'

Mandy, James and Blackie stood watching as Mr Spiller moved cautiously round to the back of the shed. Part of the wall had given way. They saw him step carefully over the rubble. As he did so his foot scraped on stone and Mandy thought she heard the wall creak. She held her breath. It seemed ages before he came out again. Mandy looked. Was he carrying something? Yes – something black and woolly.

She looked at Mr Spiller's face. He was smiling.

'He's alive?' she said.

Jack Spiller shook his head in wonder. 'I wouldn't have given tuppence for this little thing when I first saw him,' he said. 'But he's alive all right. He must be a real fighter. And look at this.'

Mandy looked at what he was holding.

'A baby's bottle,' she said.

Jack Spiller grinned. 'I reckon we've found the one that Maggie lost,' he said. 'Take this little chap into her and see if you can get some fresh milk into him. He was licking the teat of this bottle when I found him in the water trough. Lucky for him he was there and the bottle beside him. He was protected from the worst of the damage.'

'Oh!' said Mandy, taking the little creature. 'He's so frail.'

Mr Spiller scratched his head. 'I reckon he'll survive,' he said. 'After what he's been through I wouldn't put anything past him.'

James grinned. 'This is going to make Jenny get better in a hurry,' he said.

Mr Spiller grinned back. 'In that case I'd better get that shed knocked down good and proper,' he said. 'Before she gets back and starts hiding more animals in there.'

Mandy and James took the lamb into the house.

'Good heavens!' said Maggie Spiller when she

saw what they were carrying.

Once more, Mandy explained, while Mrs Spiller got some milk ready for the lamb.

'If you have any protein supplement . . .' Mandy began.

Mrs Spiller nodded. 'Your dad left some with us the other day,' she said. 'I'll get it.'

Mandy and James watched as Mrs Spiller mixed the protein supplement with the milk. Then she handed the bottle to Mandy.

'Here,' she said. 'See how much of this he'll take.'

The lamb was hungry. He sucked eagerly at the mixture in the baby's bottle and after a while his little tail began to wag.

'I really think he's going to be all right,' said Mandy.

Mrs Spiller laughed. 'Who would have thought it?' she said. 'Our Jenny will be pleased.'

Mandy smiled. Oh, yes, Jenny would be pleased.

'But I want to see him!' Jenny said.

'Just as soon as you get out of hospital,' Mandy said to her.

It was the day after the bulldozing of the shed and they were visiting Jenny.

Jenny shook her head. 'You're only saying he's

well so that I won't worry,' she said.

'No, we're not,' James said. 'He's fine, really. Your mum is feeding him and he's amazingly strong. He'll soon be able to be set on to another ewe.'

Jenny looked mutinous. 'You're just saying that,' she said again.

'Here comes Matron,' Mary Anne said from the door where she was keeping lookout. Mandy and James had sneaked past Matron's office. She hadn't seen them come in.

'Quick,' said James. 'We'll go out by the french windows.' Jenny clutched Mandy's arm. 'When will you bring Blackie?' she said.

'Hurry!' said Mary Anne.

Mandy looked at the little girl desperately. 'You know Matron won't have animals in the hospital,' she said.

'Run!' Mary Anne called.

Jenny looked at Mandy.

'Tomorrow!' Mandy said, then she leapt for the french windows.

Any moment she expected to hear a shout behind her but there was nothing.

'That was close,' said James, as they made their way round to the front of the hospital. 'How on earth are we going to get the lamb in to see Jenny?'

Mandy shrugged. 'Through the french windows, I suppose,' she said.

James looked doubtful. 'We were lucky that time,' he said. 'But I don't fancy trying to escape Matron's eagle eye very often. And what about Nurse Williams? She's always around.'

'We'll manage,' said Mandy. 'It's obvious Jenny isn't going to get better until she's seen that lamb.'

James nodded. 'At least you sound confident,' he said. 'It's more than I feel.'

But Mandy didn't feel half as confident as she sounded.

Her confidence didn't improve when she got home either.

'Gran rang,' Mrs Hope said to her.

'Oh, yes,' said Mandy.

'She wanted to know what you've been doing to upset Matron,' Mrs Hope said.

'What?' said Mandy. 'What did Gran say exactly?'

'So you *have* been up to something!' Mrs Hope said.

Mandy sighed. 'Not exactly,' she said. 'It was a mistake.'

'Hmm,' said Mrs Hope. 'I expect I should leave

well enough alone and not ask difficult questions,' she said.

Mandy looked at her mum gratefully. Mrs Hope knew that if Mandy was in real trouble she would tell her.

'Anyway,' Mrs Hope went on, 'Gran says she's got a TV crew coming tomorrow to cover the story about the hospital closure. So Matron will have other things on her mind.' Mrs Hope grinned. 'She said to let you know you could relax tomorrow at least but Matron still wanted to see you and James.'

Mandy sighed. Life was just too complicated sometimes.

'But we promised to take the lamb to see Jenny tomorrow,' James said when she told him.

Mandy nodded. 'I know,' she said. 'But how can we? If the TV crew are going to be there . . .' Then she stopped.

'What is it?' said James.

'That's just it,' said Mandy. 'The TV crew are going to be there. If we find out when they're coming then we can be sure Matron will be busy with them.'

'And we take the chance to sneak Jenny's lamb into the ward,' James said.

Mandy nodded. 'I know we aren't supposed to,' she said. 'But Matron would never listen and Jenny will go on pining until she sees her lamb.'

'So we'll just have to go for it,' said James. 'We don't have any choice, really.'

Mandy nodded in agreement.

'So how are we going to find out when the TV crew is coming?' James said.

Mandy frowned. 'I'll ask Gran. She'll be there for the filming. After all, she was the one who organised it.'

'Right,' said James. 'You go and see your Gran and I'll go up to Fordbeck Farm to see if the lamb is going to be strong enough to take tomorrow.'

Mandy nodded. 'OK,' she said. 'Let's meet at Animal Ark after tea!'

'Eleven o'clock,' Mandy said as she and James did the rounds of the animal cages in the residential unit. 'First they want an interview with Gran and Matron, then they want to film the wards and talk to the patients.'

James grinned. 'Can you imagine how pleased Mary Anne will be?' he said. 'Does she know?'

Mandy laughed. 'Of course she knows,' she said. 'Can you imagine trying to keep anything secret from Mary Anne? She was supposed to go home this morning but she asked if she could stay just one more day.'

'And Matron let her?' said James.

Mandy grinned. 'Gran pointed out to Matron that the more patients they had the better it would look.'

'Your gran is amazing,' James said.

'Gran also says that Mary Anne's mother brought her in another new nightie and a matching one for Gilda.'

James shook his head. 'She'll be a riot on TV,' he said.

'Who? Gran or Mary Anne?' said Mandy.

'Both!' James said.

'What about Blackie?' Mandy said.

'Oh, I don't think we'll take him,' said James. 'That's asking for trouble.'

'Not your Blackie, Jenny's Blackie,' Mandy said.

'Sorry,' said James. 'That lamb is amazing. He's as fit as a flea, jumping all over the place. Mr Spiller says he should have him set on in no time.'

'So he's fit to go to the hospital tomorrow?' Mandy said.

'No problem,' said James.

Not for the lamb, Mandy thought. But getting in

and out of the hospital unseen by Matron could be a big problem for them!

Twelve

Mary Anne's new nightie was bright yellow with blue polka dots.

'Do you like it?' she said to Mandy and James.

'It'll make the cameras go funny,' James said.

Mary Anne's mouth turned down.

'James is only joking,' Mandy said. 'It's lovely, Mary Anne.'

'Well, it makes my eyes go funny looking at it,' James said.

'Shh,' said Mandy. 'We're depending on Mary Anne to let us in.' She stood on tiptoe again to talk to the little girl through the open window of the children's ward.

'Remember, Mary Anne,' she said. 'Just as soon as the coast is clear, come round and open the french windows, then we can bring Jenny's lamb in to see her.'

Mary Anne nodded. 'Jenny doesn't think you're telling the truth. Is he really in there?' she said looking at the cat basket Mandy was carrying.

Mandy nodded. 'You'll see him when we bring him in,' she said.

'OK,' Mary Anne said in a whisper. She turned back into the room. 'Somebody is coming,' she said.

'You get back into bed,' said Mandy. 'We'll wait here.' She indicated a bush out of sight of the ward windows.

'I feel like a criminal,' James said.

Mandy sighed. 'Never mind,' she said. 'All we have to do is slip in, show the lamb to Jenny and slip out again. It won't take long.'

'It certainly won't,' said James. 'Not if Matron catches us. It'll be over in minutes – painfully.'

'Matron won't catch us,' said Mandy. 'She and Gran are having their interview just now. It's just a matter of waiting until Nurse Williams is out of the way.'

'*Psst!*' came a voice from the window.

Mandy and James looked up.

'Nurse Williams is in the storeroom,' Mary Anne called softly.

'OK then, open the french windows,' Mandy said.

Quickly she and James ran round to the french windows. There was the sound of a latch being lifted from inside and then Mary Anne was standing there.

'You're terrific, Mary Anne,' Mandy said as she and James stepped into the ward.

Mandy turned to Jenny's bed. A tousled head turned towards her.

'Jenny,' said Mandy. 'Look who we've brought to see you.' She opened the lid of the cat basket.

Jenny sat up, her eyes wide. 'Blackie?' she said. 'My very own Blackie?'

Mandy put the basket down on top of Jenny's bed.

'Let me see,' said Mary Anne, wriggling in front of Mandy.

'Careful,' said Mandy. 'Don't frighten him.'

'Oh, look,' said Jenny, and she lifted the little woolly lamb out of the basket.

'Hi,' said a voice from the other end of the room, 'Don't forget me.'

'I'll let Mary Anne bring him over to see you, Johnny,' Jenny said.

Mandy opened her mouth to say no, but when she looked at Jenny's face she couldn't bear to. Instead of the white face and big sad eyes, Jenny looked the picture of happiness.

'Be quick then,' said Mandy. 'We can't stay long.'

Jenny handed the little lamb to Mary Anne and Mary Anne scurried across the ward with him.

'There,' said Mary Anne and she plonked the lamb down on Johnny's bed. Its black woolly legs splayed out on either side as the lamb tried to stand up.

'He's terrific,' Johnny was saying when there was a sound in the corridor.

'Who's that?' said Mandy.

Mary Anne rushed to the door.

'Matron!' she said. 'And another lady and a man with a camera!'

'What?' said James. 'Where are they going?'

Mary Anne darted back into the room. 'I think they're coming here,' she said.

Mandy dashed across the ward, grabbed the lamb and thrust him into the cat basket. The footsteps were getting nearer. She looked across the ward. They would never get out without being seen. She backed towards the wall and found a door behind her.

'What's this?' she said.

'I don't know,' said Mary Anne.

Mandy pushed the door open. 'Come on, James,' she said. 'Get back into bed, you two, and don't say a word!'

James got the door shut just in time.

They heard voices and Nurse Williams said 'Look who's here to see you, children. Matron. And this is Mr Peters, who is going to take some pictures for the television.'

'Phew!' said James. 'That was close!'

Mandy looked round. What they needed was a way out.

'What is this place?' James whispered.

Mandy looked at the machines. 'It's the hospital laundry,' she said. 'Look, those are washing machines and dryers.'

'They're a lot bigger than ours at home,' said James.

'They would have to be,' Mandy said. 'And look at the big buckets of soap flakes.'

'Like snow,' James laughed.

Mandy frowned. There were windows in the

room but they were high up, right next to the ceiling.

'It's OK,' said James. 'They won't come in here. Why on earth would they want to come into the laundry?'

At that, the door opened and Matron's voice said, 'And this is the laundry!'

There was a scuffling sound inside the cat basket and the little black lamb leapt nimbly out.

'What on earth are you doing here, Mandy?' Gran asked. Mandy whirled round to catch the lamb, missed, and gasped in horror as it skipped into one of the buckets of soap flakes.

Scrabbling for a foothold the lamb kicked up clouds of soft white flakes which floated in the air before coming to rest all over the laundry room.

'A lamb?' said Mr Peters. 'In the laundry?'

Then Blackie got a grip on the side of the bucket and, with a kick of his heels, he was free and scampering between Matron's feet and into the ward.

'Catch him!' said James.

'Is that an animal in my hospital?' cried Matron. 'Another one?'

'Oh, Mandy,' said Gran.

In the background Jenny's voice could be heard calling to the lamb and Mary Anne was squealing with delight.

'Oh, Lord,' said James. 'We're really for it now!'

Thirteen

Matron drew herself up and looked at Mandy and James.

'You can't be cross with them,' said a small figure in a blue and yellow polka dot nightie.

Matron looked down. 'Mary Anne,' she said. 'Get back into bed at once!'

'But they only did it to make Jenny better,' said Mary Anne. 'She wasn't getting better because she was worried about her little lamb. She's much better now. It isn't fair to blame Mandy and James. They rescued her and now they've made her better.'

Mandy and James looked at her, aghast. They

would never dare to speak to Matron like that.

Mr Peters cut in before Matron could speak.

'What's this about a rescue?' he said.

Mary Anne launched into her story. There was no stopping her once she got going. Not only that, but the story was growing as she told it. Mary Anne obviously had a terrific imagination.

'She's making half of it up,' James said to Mandy. 'Sounds good though, doesn't it?'

But Mandy was listening to Mary Anne and watching Mr Peters. He had signalled to another man standing behind him, the man with the camera, and Mary Anne was being filmed while she spoke.

'This is a great story,' Mr Peters said.

At last Mary Anne ran out of steam and Mr Peters looked beyond her at the ward.

'Hey, Phil,' he said to the man with the camera, 'get a shot of the little girl with the lamb, will you?'

Mandy looked. There was Jenny with Blackie in her arms. Only he wasn't totally black any longer. He was still covered in white soap flakes. Jenny was rubbing him down with a towel.

'Hey, Matron, this is a great idea,' said Mr Peters. 'Just what we need – human interest. Pets in hospital and all that.' He turned to Matron. 'You

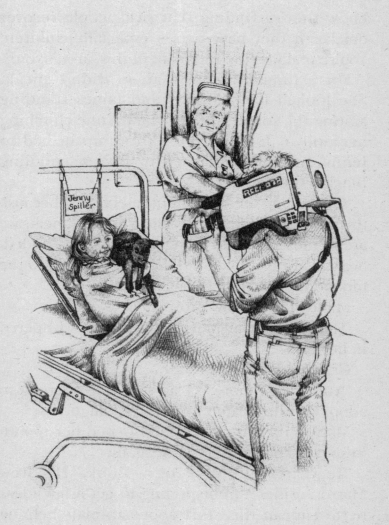

know they're finding that sick people recover
quicker if they have pets – especially children.
You're really in the forefront of this, aren't you?'

For a long moment Matron didn't speak.
She looked from Mandy and James standing
among the soap flakes to Mary Anne clutching
her doll to Johnny trying to sit up in bed to
Jenny, her face wreathed in smiles, cuddling
Blackie the lamb.

'Of course,' she said to Mr Peters. 'Just because
this is a small country hospital doesn't mean we
aren't modern. And being so small,' she added,
'we can afford to be flexible. We can cater to the
individual needs of all our patients.'

Mandy felt her jaw drop.

'She's worse than Mary Anne!' James whispered
in her ear.

Gran was smiling broadly.

'And what's more,' Gran said, 'we're going to
adopt that little lamb for our campaign.'

Matron turned to her and opened her mouth
to speak. Then she closed it again.

'Terrific,' said Mr Peters. 'Look.' He drew
Matron aside. 'I'm beginning to get a few ideas
here. I mean this stuff about animals helping
people recover is pretty interesting. Say we

combine your closure campaign with a story on how pets can aid recovery? I reckon we could get you pretty wide coverage.' He scratched his chin. 'Have you ever thought of having a pets, corner in the hospital?'

'Of course we have,' said Gran, winking at Mandy and James. 'Matron and I were just talking about that, weren't we, Matron?'

Matron looked at Gran, then she coughed. She looked across at Jenny, her head to one side. Mandy held her breath.

'You know,' Matron said, 'it's only when you see the difference this kind of thing can make to a child's recovery that you realise how important pets are to people.' She turned to Mandy and James and smiled. 'Some of us take longer to learn that than others,' she said. 'But it's a lesson not easily forgotten.'

She turned back to the television crew. 'Why don't you come to my office and we'll discuss your film? I think I can assure you that we are very seriously considering having a pets' corner at the hospital and I can think of two young people who would be ideal for running it.' She turned back and looked at Mandy and James. 'If they would take the job on,' she said.

'Would we?' said Mandy.

'You bet!' said James.

'It's like a little coat,' Jenny said.

Mr Hope and Mandy looked at each other.

'That's just what it is,' Mr Hope said.

Mandy smiled at Jenny's description. No point in telling the little girl it was the skin of a dead lamb they were putting on Blackie. Instead she said, 'It's called setting on. If we put this coat on Blackie, the ewe will think it's her own lamb and then she'll feed him.'

'But I'll still be able to come up to the field to see him,' Jenny said.

'Of course you will,' said Mr Spiller. 'He's your lamb, isn't he?'

It was two weeks after the scene at the hospital and Jenny was her old self again. She had looked after Blackie well when she had come home from hospital but now it was time for the little lamb to be put with the others in the field – if they could find a substitute mother for him.

Jenny smiled happily as they watched the ewe nuzzle Blackie and sniff suspiciously. Mandy held her breath. If the ewe wasn't fooled by the smell of her own dead lamb's coat she would reject Blackie. The ewe sniffed again. Then she nudged Blackie towards her and the little lamb started to suckle.

Mandy breathed a sigh of relief.

'It worked!' said James.

'Like a dream,' said Mr Hope. 'I reckon that's the last of your lambing problems, Jack.'

Jack Spiller turned to him. 'The end of my first lambing season. I couldn't have done it without your help,' he said. 'Not to mention these two and the people from Welford. They've been so good to us.'

'Why wouldn't they be?' said Mr Hope. 'They're neighbours, aren't they?'

Jack Spiller smiled. 'The best,' he said. 'I really feel as if I belong here now.'

Mr Hope laughed. 'That's just as well,' he said. 'Because I had it in mind to ask you to lend a hand at this year's Welford Show. And I thought you might enter Jess in the sheepdog trials.'

'I'd be delighted,' said Jack Spiller.

There was a shout from down the hill. Maggie Spiller was waving a newspaper and running up the hill towards them.

'What is it?' Jack Spiller said as she reached them.

'Look!' his wife said. 'We're famous! At least Jenny's Blackie is.'

Mandy and James craned to see what was on the front page of the paper.

The headlines stood out:

LAMB SAVES HOSPITAL

'What?' said Mandy.

Maggie Spiller laughed. 'Yes,' she said. 'It's Blackie. The cottage hospital has had a reprieve. After that TV programme went out they had hundreds of letters and phone calls. Blackie is to be the logo for a national campaign to save cottage hospitals.'

'Gosh,' said James. 'Your gran will be pleased.'

Mrs Spiller nodded. 'It says here that Mrs Dorothy Hope is to be on the national committee.'

'Good for Gran,' Mandy said. 'Isn't that terrific, Dad?'

Mr Hope ran a hand through his hair. 'I only hope Grandad can stand the pace,' he said. Then he laughed. 'Of course it's terrific. And I hope she saves lots more cottage hospitals!'

'Oh, she will,' said Mandy. 'With a logo like that, how could she fail?'

She looked at the national campaign's logo. It showed a little black lamb clutched in the arms of a child. Then she looked at Jenny, who was absorbed in watching Blackie and his new mother.

The little girl looked up. 'Blackie will always be my lamb really, won't he?' she said.

Mandy knelt down beside her. 'Of course he will, Jenny,' she said. 'Nobody loves him like you do.'

Read more about Animal Ark in
Sheepdog in the Snow

One

Christmas was coming. Mandy Hope's school had broken up for the holidays. Brightly wrapped presents were stacked under the tree in the cosy kitchen at Animal Ark, and Mandy and her friend, James Hunter, were hunched over the table surrounded by invitation cards.

'Let's make a list,' James suggested. He chewed the end of his pen. 'In alphabetical order.'

'What kind of list?' Mandy pushed her blonde hair behind her ears and scribbled away. She was making out an invitation to Gran and Grandad Hope, and Smoky the cat. Each card was hand-designed by James and Mandy. They'd cut out squares of bright yellow card, drawn the black outline of a Christmas tree on to each one, and written the words 'PARTY TIME' across the top.

'A list of guests.' James liked to be organised. He didn't want to miss anyone out. He saw Mandy was rushing into things a bit too fast. 'Shall we put pets or people first?'

'Pets,' came the prompt reply. Mandy filled out her grandparents' card. 'A Christmas Eve Party!' it read. 'Pets, bring your owners to Welford Village Hall on Saturday, 24 December at 7.30 p.m. Music and Food!' It was signed with a miniature cat's paw print, from a stencil which James had made.

'OK.' James began his list. 'Barney and Button . . . Blackie . . . Dorian . . . Eric . . . Houdini . . .' He ran through the names of some of the pets they'd helped in the past. 'Rosa won't be able to come because she's hibernating . . . but Sammy probably will, because squirrels only semi-hibernate, and—'

'Hang on a second; you missed out Ruby and Prince.' Mandy remembered the piglet and the pony as she tucked the invitation into an envelope.

'Hmm . . . Can we get a pony into the village hall?' James wondered.

Mandy thought carefully. 'I suppose Susan could bring him and stay outside with him. Prince could stick his head through an open window and enjoy things from there.'

'And what about pigs?'

She imagined cheeky, adventurous Ruby trotting in and out of the trestle-tables, rooting for food. She nodded. 'Pigs are fine. We want everyone to come, remember. It's going to be the biggest, best Christmas party for pets anyone's ever seen!'

Mandy's blue eyes shone. Animals were the love of her life, and the idea of giving them a Christmas treat, where all the past patients of Animal Ark could get together with pets which Mandy and James had helped to rescue, and farm animals they'd managed to save, promised to make this a Christmas to remember.

She imagined everyone gathered there; cats and dogs, rabbits, hamsters, sheep and pigs. She wanted to invite Ernie Bell and his squirrel, Sammy, Lydia Fawcett and her wonderful escaping goat, Houdini. She even wanted Pandora the Pekinese and Toby the mongrel, though this would mean having to invite their fussy owner, Mrs Ponsonby. 'I wonder if Pandora will come in fancy dress?' Mandy smiled.

'No, but I expect Mrs Ponsonby will.' James hitched his glasses further up his nose. He slotted

Pandora's name into the list. 'Hey, let's have a competition for the best party hat!' he suggested.

'And carols. And a Christmas procession down the village street.' Mandy could picture the magic scene. For a few moments she stopped to daydream. She'd take along Mopsy, the tamest of her three rabbits, warmly zipped up inside the front of her jacket. They would have to draw up a menu of food, from lettuce leaves for Mopsy to oats for Susan Price's pony. It would be snowing outside, and they would carry candles down the street. They would crowded into the village hall, singing carols. Then the pets would be let loose on the party food . . .

'Mandy?' James broke in.

'Hmm?'

'I said, do you want to invite Imogen with Button and Barney, or John Hardy?'

'Both,' Mandy beamed. She was feeling generous. 'You know, Imogen Parker Smythe isn't nearly so spoiled now she has the two rabbits to look after. In fact, I'd even say she was quite nice!'

'And what about Claire?' James remembered his little, dark-haired, next-door neighbour. She ran a hedgehog sanctuary in her garden. 'Rosa, Guy and everyone will be fast asleep for the winter in their next-boxes.'

Mandy's brow wrinkled. 'Yes, we can't wake them up specially, just to come to a party. Claire will have to come by herself.' She began to make out a fresh invitation. It was only five days until Christmas Eve, and they had loads to do.

In the background, they could hear Adam Hope, Mandy's dad, pottering about the house. He went up and downstairs, in and out of the lounge, humming and singing to himself. Then he put his bearded face round the kitchen door.

> *Christmas is coming,*
> *The goose is getting fat . . .*

he sang;

> *Please put a penny*
> *In the old man's hat.*
> *If you haven't got a penny,*
> *A halfpenny will do.*
> *If you haven't got a halfpenny,*
> *A farthing will do.*
> *If you haven't got a farthing . . .*

'*God bless you!*' Mandy and James chimed in, their faces wreathed in smiles.

If you like *Animal Ark*® then you'll love *Animal Action!*
Subscribe for just **£8** and you can look forward to six
issues of *Animal Action* magazine, throughout the year.
Each issue of *Animal Action* is bursting with animal
news and features, competitions and fun and games! Plus,
when you subscribe, you'll become a free *Animal Action*
Club member too, so we'll send you a fab joining pack
and FREE donkey notepad and pen!

To subscribe, simply complete the form below – a photocopy is fine – and send it with a
cheque for £8 (made payable to RSPCA) to RSPCA Animal Action Club, Wilberforce Way,
Southwater, Horsham, West Sussex RH13 9RS.

Don't delay, join today!

Name:

Address:

Postcode: Date of birth:

Signature of parent/guardian:

Data Protection Act: This information will be held on computer and used only by the RSPCA.
Please allow 28 days for delivery. **AACHOD07**